DEAD SALVATION

OTHER LIVING DEAD PRESS BOOKS

TWISTED FISH: AN AQUATIC ANTHOLOGY
THE DEAD OF SPACE BOOK 1 AND 2
PLANET OF THE DEAD
DREAM WEAVERS
THE JUNKYARD
THE HAUNTED THEATRE
UNITED STATES OF ARMAGEDDON
HALLOWEEN TALES OF TERROR
DROPPING FEAR
CHUPACABRA VISIONS
PLAYING GOD: A ZOMBIE NOVEL
THE TURNING: A STORY OF THE LIVING DEAD
JUST BEFORE NIGHT: A ZOMBIE ANTHOLOGY
THE BOOK OF HORROR * KNIGHT SYNDROME
THE WAR AGAINST THEM: A ZOMBIE NOVEL
CHILDREN OF THE VOID * DARK DREAMS
BLOOD RAGE & DEAD RAGE (BOOK 1& 2 OF THE RAGE VIRUS SERIES)
DEAD MOURNING: A ZOMBIE HORROR STORY
BOOK OF THE DEAD: A ZOMBIE ANTHOLOGY VOLUME 1-5
LOVE IS DEAD: A ZOMBIE ANTHOLOGY
ETERNAL NIGHT: A VAMPIRE ANTHOLOGY
END OF DAYS: AN APOCALYPTIC ANTHOLOGY VOLUME 1-4
DEAD HOUSE: A ZOMBIE GHOST STORY
THE ZOMBIE IN THE BASEMENT (FOR ALL AGES)
THE LAZARUS CULTURE: A ZOMBIE NOVEL
DEAD WORLDS: UNDEAD STORIES VOLUMES 1-7
FAMILY OF THE DEAD, REVOLUTION OF THE DEAD
RANDY AND WALTER: PORTRAIT OF TWO KILLERS
KINGDOM OF THE DEAD * DEAD HISTORY
THE MONSTER UNDER THE BED * DEAD THINGS
DEAD TALES: SHORT STORIES TO DIE FOR
ROAD KILL: A ZOMBIE TALE * DEADFREEZE * DEADFALL
SOUL EATER * THE DARK * RISE OF THE DEAD
DEAD END: A ZOMBIE NOVEL * VISIONS OF THE DEAD
THE CHRONICLES OF JACK PRIMUS
INSIDE THE PERIMETER: SCAVENGERS OF THE DEAD
THE DEADWATER SERIES
DEADWATER * DEADWATER: Expanded Edition
DEADRAIN * DEADCITY * DEADWAVE * DEAD HARVEST
DEAD UNION * DEAD VALLEY * DEAD TOWN * DEAD GRAVE
DEAD SALVATION
COMING SOON
BOOK OF CANNIBALS VOLUME 2
DEAD ARMY (Deadwater series book 10)
EMAILS OF THE DEAD: A ZOMBIE ANTHOLOGY
CHRISTMAS IS DEAD VOLUME 2

DEAD SALVATION

BOOK 9

ANTHONY GIANGREGORIO

DEAD SALVATION

WHAT HAS COME BEFORE

Two years ago, a deadly bacterial outbreak escaped a lab to infect the lower atmosphere across America, unleashing an undead plague on the world.

With rain clouds now filled with a killer bacteria, to venture outside in the rain was tantamount to suicide.

To get caught in the rain and exposed to the bacteria would be an instant death. But that wasn't the end. Once dead, the host body would rise again, becoming an undead ghoul, wanting nothing more than to feed on the flesh of the living.

Eventually, the bacteria burned off in the atmosphere but mankind still wasn't safe. The virus then mutated inside the host, and to be bitten by one of the living dead was a death sentence. Sickness followed by a painful death, only to return as one of the undead.

The United States was torn asunder; civilization collapsing like a house of cards in the weeks after the dead began to walk.

But mankind survived, eking out a dreary existence, always keeping one eye open for the attacking dead.

Only two years after the zombie apocalypse, the world has become a very different place from what it once was. Gone are cell phones, the internet, restaurants and shopping malls; now all lost relics of a culture slowly fading into history.

In this new world, the dead walk and a man follows the rules of the gun, where the strong are always right and the weak are usually dead. Major cities are nothing but blackened husks, nothing but giant tombs filled with walking corpses.

Across America, smaller towns have become small municipalities with makeshift walls protecting them from both living and undead attackers. Strangers are not welcome and are either shot on sight or made to move on, that is, if they are not exploited by the rulers of the towns.

Through the destruction of what once was walks a man, crushing death beneath his steel-tipped boots. Before, he was an ordinary man, living a quiet life with a wife and a career, but the rules have changed and so too, has he adapted, becoming a warrior of death who wields a gun with an iron hand, but shows mercy and wisdom when it is needed.

His name is Henry Watson, and with his fellow companions, Mary, Jimmy, Cindy, Sue and Raven by his side, he travels across a blighted landscape, searching for someplace where the undead haven't corrupted everything they touch; where he can lay his head down in safety.

Though life is fleeting, each breath means the possibility of one more day of life, and a better future for all.

Prologue

The road was nothing special. It could be a road from anyplace in the United States, or the new name given to the country by the survivors—deadlands.

Here, there were zombies, two kinds mostly. There were deaders, which were the standard zombie, the ones that never left where they were first reborn as ghouls.

The second were called roamers. These were zombies that traveled across the country, seeking food—human of course—and weren't content to stay in one place for too long.

As if the walking dead weren't enough, another threat soon appeared to plague the land.

Cannibals.

Or cannies for short.

Many humans, too lazy to forage or grow their own food, had taken to eating one another instead. The lowest form of life, they were a pox on what was good and were a terror to all not able to withstand them.

With filed teeth and unwashed bodies, in many ways they were worse than the ghouls, for these humans *knew* what they were doing, and didn't just operate on instinct.

They chose to feed on other humans as an easy solution to the food problem of the new America.

With civilization in the crapper, no trucks transported food across the country, and people had to learn to fend for themselves.

Henry Watson and his group of warrior survivalists had come across cannies many times, and each time had managed to destroy the tribe.

Knowing how deadly they were, Henry vowed to wipe them from the face of the planet, one evil bastard at a time.

So far, he had made good on his promise, leaving a wake of corpses in his back trail.

Until now.

Chapter 1

"You think we can take them?" Jimmy Cooper asked as he peered through the battered binoculars at the road below. He was in his early twenties, with wild brown hair and a wiry frame. While he had grown over the past two years, he still had a way of wise-cracking most of the time. By his side was a pump-action shotgun, and a Bowie knife road his hip.

"Don't see as we've got a choice," Henry Watson replied askance of him. "And we have surprise on our side." His powerful frame was stretched out in the grass, his hard muscles undeniable under his clothing. Two years of living on the run, fighting to survive, had chiseled his once doughy form into a mass of raw muscle and tendons. His skin, once a deep dark tan, was still a light brown, even after spending time on the mountains of Colorado. On his left hip was strapped a sixteen inch panga, the blade honed to a razor's edge. On his right hip was his trusty 9mm Glock, the clip loaded with steel-jacketed rounds. The gun held a total of eighteen rounds; seventeen in the clip and one in the chamber. Though the stopping power wasn't as great as other caliber guns, the side arm had been with him from the start, and he valued it greatly.

"Yeah, Henry, but is that enough to do this without getting killed?" Mary Roberts asked from his left. She was tall and slim, with brown hair hanging past her shoulders. Her cheekbones gave her the look of a duchess, or a princess, but she was all woman. On her hip rode a .38 Smith and Wesson, the revolver loaded and ready for action.

"It's gonna have to be," Henry replied. He cast a glance to Cindy Jansen, who was next to Mary, her lithe form spread out in the tall grass. "You think you can take out at least three of 'em on your own?"

"No problem, Henry," Cindy grinned as she brushed her long blonde hair away from her face. She had the figure of a runway model, with a thin waist, plump hips, and firm breasts. Her skin was as smooth as spider silk and her deep blue eyes burned with a fire that was impossible to suppress.

She leaned forward and peered through the small scope on her M16, gauging the distance to the targets below. On her hip was a .45, the gun cleaned and oiled with a full clip. "I can probably get four of 'em if I'm lucky."

Henry nodded. "I don't care about luck, Cindy. This is about exacts. You take out three and that'll leave the other six for the rest of us. We can each take two a piece. With skill and planning, this should go down without any casualties on our side."

"Aww, come on, old man, a little luck isn't a bad thing," Jimmy quipped as he handed the binoculars to Henry.

Henry frowned as he ran his hand through his gray hair and scratched his chin, then peered through the binoculars.

"Maybe you're right, Jimmy, but still, I'd rather not count on it to see us through this thing." He glanced to Cindy again. "How's your ankle?"

"I'll be fine in a couple of days. But I can still shoot."

"Can't wait to get 'em," Raven said as she flicked her hands in the air. Her fingernails were razor sharp and could slice a man's throat open before he knew what was happening. Her long, ebony hair seemed to soak up the light as she kneeled before Henry, her jaw firm, her eyes cold. She was a born killing machine, and Henry sometimes wondered how she came to be. Before the dead walked, Raven would have been an ordinary girl. So if that was so, then how could she be so deadly? What was her story? The girl never spoke much and her past was a mystery.

"No, Raven, I want you to stay behind with Cindy," Henry told her.

Raven opened her mouth to protest, as she always did, but Henry stopped her cold by bringing his arm up, then down in a chopping motion. "I said no, dammit, no arguing. You don't have a gun and I don't want you down there without one."

"Don't need one," she said curtly.

"Maybe so, and you've proved you don't need one, but still, I don't want you down there without a weapon." His voice softened. "You want to carry a gun?"

She shook her head.

"Fine, then it's settled."

"What about me, Henry?" Sue Anders asked from his opposite side. She was in her early forties but was still a stunning woman to behold, with blonde hair and eyes that rivaled Cindy's in their intensity. On her hip, she carried a small .22 handgun. For the moment, it was all Henry trusted her to use.

Henry turned to look at Sue, his heart softening the second his eyes made contact with hers. Since he lost his wife, Emily, two years ago at the beginning of the zombie outbreak, he believed he would never love again. He had wrestled with that very subject for quite a while, and finally had come to peace with the loss of his wife.

And now he had Sue, and he loved her as much as he loved Emily. It felt good to think that, he knew. It was freeing. Besides, Emily had been his old life, Sue was his new one. The one where the dead walked.

"You stay here, too," he told her. "We both know you're no good down there with us."

She nodded, knowing he was correct. While slowly becoming a warrior with each passing day, Sue still had a long way to go before she was as tough and battle-hardened as the rest of the companions.

"Okay, good, we wait for sunset," Henry said. "Then we hit them just after dark when they've eaten and are a little slow and lazy. Until then, everyone try to grab some rest, I'll keep watch until it's time."

Everyone said they were fine with his orders and each stretched out on the tall grass on the hill overlooking the road. All six of them knew to take rest when they could. At any moment, danger could arrive to have them fighting for their lives, whether it was human or the walking dead.

So far, the undead hadn't been prominent since leaving the mountains of Colorado. After dealing with the snow in the high altitude, it was a pleasant respite to return to sea level, even if that meant they had to deal with the undead once more

They had spent a few days in a nameless town, resting and re-cuperating, especially Henry who'd had to fight for his life when they stumbled upon a house in the woods, filled with a family of cannibals that had wanted to make Henry and his group their next meal.

Obviously he and the others had won the day, but not without Henry catching a couple more wounds to add to the dozens he'd already received. When the wounds healed, he would have more scars to add to the patchwork criss-crossing his muscular body.

Henry peered through the tall grass at the small cannie convoy below as they made camp for the night. As he watched, he had to fight himself not to jump up, run down the hill, and kill them all single-handedly

It was about a year ago that the first cannibal tribes appeared. The Crystal shopping mall was the companions first run in with cannibalism, but now they were a blight on the entire country.

Which was what brought the companions to the hill overlooking the deserted road filled with cannies below.

The six companions were twenty miles north of Interstate 40, and after traveling for more than a day, Cindy had managed to trip in a hole in the ground, perhaps from some burrowing creature. They had been crossing a field when it happened.

At first Cindy thought she was fine, but when she tried to walk, blinding pain had shot up her leg.

After inspecting the ankle, it was decided it was a slight sprain and would be fine in a few days, but the area they were in wasn't very safe.

Needing to keep moving, Jimmy and Henry began carrying her, but after the first few miles, both men were exhausted, the extra weight of Cindy, combined with their backpacks, was simply too much for them. Mary tried to help but she was already loaded down with a full load of gear.

And then fortune had found them in the shape of a cannibal convoy which had begun to set up for the night on the empty back road.

There were two vehicles in the convoy, one, an old Datsun, and the other was a pickup truck. Since the world went to hell in an undead handbasket, pickup trucks were one of the most versatile vehicles a person could use. Their frames were usually high off the road with thick tires and the back beds had a thousand uses, including fitting a dozen or more men at a time.

In the cannies' case, they had five prisoners in the rear bed of the pickup truck—all of them tied up with rope—two men, a woman, and two children, a boy and a girl.

From watching the prisoners, the companions were fairly certain they were all a family with the exception of the extra man. This man looked ex-military, with a tight haircut and clean-shaven face. If a man was traveling on the road, he would rarely shave, as was the countenance of the other man, the father.

But the military man had a clean face, which said he was within a day's travel of someplace where he had cleaned up and shaved.

As far as the companions knew, there was nothing close. No towns but the one they'd left behind, and there was no way the man could have been there, then left, to have been captured by the cannies all in that small amount of time.

So he had to be from somewhere else; where didn't matter at the moment.

Though the cannies had five prisoners which they would use for food, that wasn't the reason Henry had decided to hit the convoy. Of course, he didn't mind saving a few lives as he met his own needs also, but this still wasn't the deciding factor.

It was the pickup truck.

With the pickup in the companions' possession, they could travel in style and Cindy could stay off her bad ankle. Transportation in an undead world was as valuable as gold once was, the shiny metal now worthless. If you couldn't eat it, snort it, drink it, fuck it, or shoot it, then what the hell was it good for?

So he planned on hitting the convoy, killing the despicable cannies, saving the prisoners, and taking the pickup truck for his group all in one whack.

He glanced to his side to see Jimmy already sleeping, his mouth partially open as he snored lightly, his .38 S&W in his right hand, both resting on his stomach. Henry glanced to the nine inch Bowie knife and the shotgun, the weapon cleaned and oiled and ready for action.

Henry grinned as he watched his young friend sleep. He thought back to when he'd first met him and how young and a pain in the ass he was. Now Jimmy was a warrior, a man Henry was proud to call a friend. And only a true warrior could sleep upon going into battle. In the two years and a handful of months he'd been traveling with Jimmy, the two had become good friends, closer to a father and son relationship than he'd ever care to admit. He shifted slightly, feeling the bump of his Glock and panga. He reached down out of instinct, feeling the Glock on his right hip and the panga on his left, riding a little low for a fast draw. He'd practiced for many hours on how to reach down and slide the sixteen inch blade out of its sheathe in less than a second, and once he'd mastered the skill, he'd put it to good use on more than one occasion. The severed heads of the undead across the country could attest to that.

Glancing to his left, he listened to Mary and Cindy talking softly.

Mary had her .38 resting in front of her, her hand on the grip, while Cindy lay on her stomach, her eye still peering through the scope of her rifle. She was still watching the cannie convoy, her mind placing each shot for when she had her chance to shoot. Cindy also carried a six inch hunting knife strapped to her belt and she knew how to use it with deadly accuracy as more than one man could attest to, the scars a grim reminder they had messed with the wrong woman. And this had happened more times than the companions could count when they were inside towns and forts. With Cindy's hair a golden blonde and her figure that of a super model, her tight denim jeans and polo shirt, the latter showing off her well formed breasts, she made every man she met drool with desire.

But Cindy had eyes for only one man and that was Jimmy. For some unknown reason, Cindy found Jimmy's wisecracks and quips endearing, plus she thought he was cute. A .45 pistol rode her hip though she rarely used it, preferring the M16 instead. She was a crack shot and had saved the group more than once with her marksmanship.

Henry shifted position, getting more comfortable. There was a cool breeze blowing, rustling the nearby trees, and cooling his sweaty brow. It was times like this, as he waited to go into a battle, he always found it so amazing that only two years ago he was a regular guy with a job and a wife. Now he was as close to a mercenary as you could get, a warrior of the new world.

It had been simple, really, adapt or die and he had chosen the former, and so too, did his friends.

The world was a very different place now, the country transformed into a hellscape of the walking dead who ate the living. And the human cannibals only added to the evil, but where the dead were unstoppable, their numbers massive, the cannibals weren't, and Henry had already vowed to wipe then from the face of the earth one cannie at a time. The only question being, whether that was sooner or later. He had no doubt he would do it, even if it took every day of the rest of his life. Sometimes he imagined himself at seventy, roaming the deadlands and fighting zombies and cannies. If he was able, that would be his future.

The next three hours went by slowly, Jimmy snoring, Mary catching an hour or so, but Henry and Cindy stayed alert, both waiting for the time to fight.

Sunset cast the camp, road, and the overlooking hill the companions were on, in gloom as the sun gave up the fight for another day. Another hour and Henry would gather his people and go on the attack, but he didn't realize that things were about to deviate from the original plan.

It was as Mary was waking up from her catnap that she heard a high-pitched scream, then Henry and Cindy heard it a second later. It was coming from the cannies' camp, but in the shifting shadows by the road, it was hard to see.

"Something's happening down there," Cindy said, her eye on her rifle scope, while Jimmy snored next to her. She had once said she thought he could sleep through WW3 if no one bothered to wake him to tell him it was the end of the world.

"Doesn't sound good," Henry said. "What do you see, Cindy?"

Cindy adjusted the scope to compensate for the fading light, and as she did this, she frowned. "Shit, it looks like they got one of the kids, the little girl." Her voice was going up some, indicating she didn't like what she saw. "They're dragging her to the middle of the camp, near the fire."

Mary moved closer. "What are they doing to her? She sounds scared."

Cindy didn't reply and Henry was about to prod Cindy when the blonde woman spoke up again. "Oh, shit, guys, I think she's gonna be dinner!"

"Oh my God, no," Sue whispered beside Henry as Raven flexed her arms for a fight.

"What! Move over, let me see," Mary demanded and pushed her out of the way. Cindy squeaked a little at the shove but she let Mary use the scope. She glanced to Henry who only smiled slightly. He knew how Mary could get so didn't say a word.

"Hey, what the hell, guys? I thought we were gonna get some rest? The sun is barely down," Jimmy croaked as he looked about with blurry eyes.

"Something's happening at the camp," Cindy told him. "One of the kids might be in trouble."

That got him awake and he sat up. "Oh shit, really? Oh, Christ, those fuckers aren't gonna..." He trailed off, not wanting to say it.

Cindy nodded. "Yeah, baby, I think that's what might be happening."

Mary was squinting through the scope as she studied the camp. There was the pickup truck, and the Datsun with its doors wide open, while men and women moved about, preparing for the evening meal.

The only trouble was that the meal wasn't going to be canned beans and fruit cocktail, the meal was going to be the slaughtered carcass of the little girl.

Mary sighted in on a grizzly bear-looking man with black hair covering every part of his body besides his neck and forehead. He had a thick beard that went down to the middle of his chest and wore a pair of dark jeans with a white t-shirt that was so dirty from stains and sweat it was now brown. He held a cleaver in his right hand and in his left was the little girl, the man's meaty fist clenched in her hair.

Tears were in the child's eyes and her mouth was open, the shrieks of fear escaping like bubbles from a sinking ship.

"My God, Henry," Sue exclaimed. "They're going to kill that little girl, we need to do something!"

"There's nothing we can do, Sue, not yet anyway," Henry told her.

As Mary watched the tableau play out, she could hear Henry talking beside her.

"Mary, you need to let it go," he said. "It's terrible what's happening, but we can't save everyone. It's too early to go down there. We need to wait for it to get darker. You're just going to have to accept that the little girl is d..."

He never got to finish his sentence because at that exact moment, Mary lined up the hairy cannie's head in the rifle's sights and fired, sending a 5.56 mm round into the man's head.

As the report of the shot rang out across the hillside, down in the camp, the cannie's head disintegrated in a wash of bone and brain matter. The hand holding the little girl twitched and then let go as death spasms rocked the now headless body. A geyser of blood shot out from the neck wound to dance across the road, drenching the little girl in warm plasma. The other hand, the one with the cleaver, spun in a circle before the cleaver dropped to the pavement with a dull metal *clang*.

As the hairy cannie's body dropped to the road, the legs still jumping up and down as nerves died, the little girl fell to the pavement, screaming for her mommy. All around her, the other cannies dove for cover, realizing they were under fire after seeing their leader's head disappear in a massive explosion of gore.

Gunfire was returned to the top of the hill, where the companions quickly found themselves pinned down.

"Shit, Mary, why in God's name did you have to go and do that?" Henry yelled as he fired off a few shots at the cannies, who were now hiding behind their two vehicles for cover.

In the darkness, he couldn't see his targets and only tried to keep them honest, not wanting to give them a chance to rush up the hill at the group. It would be easy for the cannies to send a few of their tribe to circle around the side of the hill and take the companions from behind or out flank them.

To Henry's right, Jimmy was firing down the hill with his .38. His shotgun sat beside him, but for now it was useless, the distance too great for the shells to do any good. But if he moved closer it would see some use.

Cindy had taken back her M16 with an annoyed look at Mary, who only smiled wanly, not really apologizing, but still not wanting her friend to be mad at her.

Cindy dropped down and sighted the cannies through the scope, looking for a target. In the campfire, she could see the shadows of people hiding behind the vehicles but so far she didn't have a shot. Then one of the cannies figured out the campfire was a beacon for gunfire and a woman with long filthy hair ran out with a bucket of water. As she tossed the water onto the campfire, dousing it, Cindy took her shot.

The bullet caught the cannie woman in the upper right shoulder, blowing out a large piece of her flesh and bone. She went down and stayed down, though Cindy could see her trying to crawl back behind cover.

"Oh, no, you don't," Cindy muttered under her breath as she sighted on the woman's back as the wounded cannie wormed her way across the pavement.

Taking her time, Cindy waited for the woman to be within inches of safety, and then she fired, just as another cannie—a man—jumped out to grab the woman.

The helper cannie managed to grab the woman by the hands and then the woman's body seemed to jump an inch off the road as the round from the rifle smacked into her back, sending her face first into the pavement where she bounced once.

The helper cannie, realizing the woman was dead, jumped back behind cover just as a round ricocheted off the pavement an inch from him. But then the man was hidden and Cindy had lost her chance to take him out. Cursing her luck, she pressed her eye to the scope tighter and waited for another target to appear.

In the nearby woods, just off the road, a pack of ghouls had been moving about. Aimlessly at first, they heard the gunshots and like a moth to a flame, began to move in that direction.

In less than five minutes they were at the edge of the road, coming up on the cannies from behind. On the hill, Cindy, with her scope was the first one to spot the movement of the zombies.

For the past five minutes the gunfight had raged, sometimes faltering as each group tried to reload while others covered them. A few times two of the cannies tried to run to the side to outflank the companions, but Cindy kept them in check with a few, well-placed rounds. One time she scored a hit, clipping a cannie with a pony-tail in the right leg. Even over the gunfire, she heard the outcry of pain as the cannie lost a chunk of his leg.

But it wasn't a killing shot, and a few minutes later the man was firing back at the companions, albeit now with a hastily applied bandage.

"Henry!" Cindy cried. "There's movement behind the truck, can you see it?"

Henry peered into the falling darkness, and as he relaxed and let his eyes pick up the shifting shadows; he did spot the slow, plodding forms of the zombies.

There were eight in all, which in normal circumstances wouldn't be much of a threat to the cannies, but now, with a gun-fight ongoing and some of their number already down, this could be the advantage the companions needed.

Jimmy scored a hit, catching an older cannie with a round to the shoulder. The old man fell down, but a minute later was back, now firing with his wounded arm so his free one could staunch the flow of blood from the wound. Despite hating the cannies as much as Henry, Jimmy had to give the wounded man a pat on the back for courage. They may be degenerates, but they were brave in the face of battle.

Still, Jimmy would reward the man for his stamina by putting a bullet to his head, if he had the chance.

Sue was hunkered low beside Henry as was Raven. The young girl's face was scrunched up in anger and all she wanted to do was run down there and slice up the cannies.

Off to the right, Jimmy cast a glance at Mary. She was scowling as she shot at the cannie convoy. Even in the darkness, he was able to catch glimpse of her face when she fired from the muzzle flash, and each time, he didn't like what he saw. She looked hurt and concerned, as she was wont to do when others were in danger.

Mary was the conscience of the companions; she would do the right thing even if it put them all in mortal danger. There were times when she had almost cost them their lives because of her moral compass, but despite this, the group loved and respected her, realizing that whatever had created this new world of death, somehow hadn't gotten its hooks into Mary—at least not yet.

She was as pure and noble as the day the outbreak first began.

Down below, on the road, the zombies reached the cannies.

At first the cannies thought they were being attacked by more humans, but soon realized it was the undead.

This caused a hell of a distraction as the cannies now had to shoot the ghouls while still being careful not to step out into the open where they would be exposed and shot by the companions.

Pony-tail cannie made this mistake, and when he backed away from a zombie, and inadvertently moved from the cover of the pickup truck, Cindy put a round into the side of his torso, causing the man to cry out and fall to the road.

Not a kill shot, he dropped hard, and no sooner did he land, blood seeping from the wound, then the zombie he was trying to escape from pounced on him, pale and cracked fingers reaching into the opening of the bullet hole to tear his flesh from his bones.

His anguished screams of death filled the road, chilling even the cannies' cold hearts, as he was devoured alive.

"It looks like we got ourselves some help!" Henry called out to the others as he dropped down lower and changed his spent clip. The seventeen round clips were as valuable as gold to him, for without them he would be loading one bullet at a time.

Sliding the spent clip into his pocket, he slapped a new one in and primed the gun. The Glock had been with him from the beginning and was as much a part of him as his arm or leg. Though just a gun, it was one of the last things he had left of his past, of who he once was, and he took excellent care of it.

And the gun had saved his life more times than he could count.

Down on the road, the cannies were more than a match for the ghouls and for a few brief seconds, they ignored the companions as they began firing at their undead attackers.

Henry was prepared to wait the cannies out, letting them expel as much ammunition on the walking dead and suffer casualties, as they could manage when Mary suddenly jumped up and began running down the hill.

"Mary, where the hell are you going?" Henry screamed.

"The girl!" Mary replied. "She's in danger from a deader! I didn't start all this to see her killed now!" And then she was running down the hill, for all purposes looking like a young girl playing on a hill after school, her arms out to her sides as she fought to keep her balance in the tall grass.

"I don't believe this!" Henry snapped and climbed to his feet as he grabbed Jimmy by the scruff of his shirt. "Jimmy, come on, we can't let her go down there alone!"

Jimmy didn't reply, he only jumped up with Henry's help and the two took off down the hill.

"Cindy, watch our backs!" Henry yelled over his shoulder. "And Raven, you stay put!"

"I gotcha covered, be careful," Cindy called as she peered through her scope at the convoy below. Raven pouted, crossing her arms over her chest in frustration. "This sucks," she said.

Henry barely heard her reply, the wind whistling through his ears as he and Jimmy barreled down the hill to catch up to Mary. And that was proving harder than he thought.

The ground was uneven under the tall grass and his footing was precarious. In the darkness, he was almost blind and he expected to fall head first at any moment.

Jimmy was dealing with the same problem. His .38 was holstered now, the shotgun in his hands, held out in front of him like a balancing bar, as his knees went up and down as he ran over the uneven terrain.

But both were managing to stay upright and in the end that's what mattered.

Mary was quicker on her feet. Like a deer, she glided over the terrain and straight for the cannie camp.

As she approached the camp, the pale starlight illuminated the convoy a little more and she spotted the little girl again.

It had been seconds since Mary had seen the shadow appear behind the screaming girl and Mary began running down the hill, but in that time the shambling form had grown so close it leered over the small girl.

Mary knew she had one chance, one shot at saving the girl's life.

If she missed, the ghoul looming over the girl would attack. And she knew the grisly result if that happened.

As she entered the small camp, she took in the shifting forms around her. In the darkness, ghoul and cannie were one and the same, only the voices of the cannies cursing differentiating the figures.

Her .38 was already up, and as the ghoul leaned down to sink fetid teeth into the screaming girl, Mary fired, the range no more than ten feet.

At first she couldn't tell if she had hit her target, but a second later the ghoul was gone, and the girl was screaming even more as the zombie's congealed blood, cold and sticky, splashed onto her head from the impact of lead to dead flesh.

Mary swooped in and ran up to the girl, scooping her up in her arms. As she turned to run, to escape the maelstrom of chaos she now found herself in, she turned and found herself staring at the dead faces of two zombies.

Even in the pale darkness suffusing the road, she could see these two were an ugly looking pair. One had no nose and was missing an eye, the gaping socket like a small cavern. The other had almost no face at all, only a rotting pile of meat where yellow bone peered through amongst the decayed flesh. Maggots squirmed in the meat, some falling out to land on the road to be crushed, while others crawled in and out of every orifice in the ghoul's face, like an all you can eat snack bar for larva.

Mary took a step backward but as she did, she felt the muzzle of a gun in her back.

Glancing over her shoulder, she stared into the dark eyes of a cannie, the man's face so covered in dirt she couldn't make out his features. Only his pointed teeth, though yellow, reflected what ambient light was available. His eyes, which seemed to glow in his head like two marbles, reflected each muzzle flash going off around him.

"Well, well, looks like we got us some Grade-A meat," he growled as he prepared to squeeze the trigger and send Mary on the last train west.

"Whatever the dead fucks leave behind will be great in the stew pot," he breathed. "You look as tender as they get," he smirked as his finger began to squeeze the trigger and send Mary to Hell.

Mary had never feared death, and the little girl in her arms had become her charter and it broke her heart to think she had failed the crying girl. But she knew when her number was up, and though it made her scream inside, she accepted her fate.

All this flew through her head in less than half a second. As she closed her eyes and waited to feel the sharp kiss of the cannie's bullet penetrate her back, her entire body jumped an inch into the air when her ears heard the gunshot that would finally end her life.

Chapter 2

Mary gasped, expecting to feel a bullet slice through her organs, but instead of feeling the intense pain of lead penetrating her back, she felt warm blood splatter the side of her face. Spinning around, she saw the cannie falling to the road, a bullet hole seeping red in the middle of his forehead, the back of his skull now gone. Mary cast a glance the other way to see Henry—his Glock still aimed at the fallen cannie—and Jimmy reaching the road, climbing over the guardrail to help her.

She waved thanks, realizing Henry had saved her yet again, and grabbed the little girl, moving off to find a safe place wait out the battle.

Jimmy and Henry ran directly between the two vehicles, their guns aimed at whatever moved. The advantage was there were only enemies to shoot, so they never had to pause to make sure, unlike the cannies who didn't want to shoot one another.

There were six cannies and half a dozen ghouls left moving about the camp, and Jimmy took out two cannies with a blast to their stomachs. Gut shot, the two men fell over, their intestines sliding out of their stomachs like coils of greasy rope. Jimmy was about to put them out of their misery when two zombies appeared from behind the Datsun and pounced on the screaming men, sinking their pale hands into the open bullet wounds of the cannies' abdomens.

Jimmy watched for all of ten seconds before he shot both ghouls in the head, then finished off the still screaming cannies.

Pumping the shotgun, he spun to see what else he could shoot. He spotted Henry's dark shape moving through the camp and then a woman cannie came out of the shadows, a large kitchen knife in her hand. Jimmy was ready to yell out to Henry to watch his back, when the older warrior, as if he sensed the danger, spun on the balls of his feet and shot the woman in the chest.

The cannie, her dirt-crusted hair waving in the wind, went flying backwards as her arms began spinning in circles. But she couldn't keep herself up and she fell heavily into the extinguished fire, the coals still hot despite the dousing earlier. She rolled on the ground, her back now seared as the scent of cooked flesh filled the road, a few coals burning deeply into her flesh.

Disgusted, Henry shot her in the face, ending her suffering. He could have cared less that she was a woman. She was a cannie—that went beyond gender.

Henry searched for another target and he saw the prisoners of the cannies were in trouble. Tied up in the truck bed, their hands were useless to fend off the attacking ghouls.

As Henry took a few steps closer to the pickup truck, he saw the bearded man and the other, clean-shaven man, use their feet to try and kick the ghouls back, hoping to keep them away, but when you were fighting an undead foe that felt no pain, it was all but useless.

The bearded man was grabbed by his right foot by a zombie and yanked off his feet, the woman and boy screaming in fear for him. Henry lined up a shot, wanting to take the zombie down, but even as he fired, the ghoul sank its teeth into the bearded man's leg.

Then the bullet struck the side of the ghoul's head, going right into its ear, and blowing out the opposite side of its head. With the bearded man's leg still in its mouth, the zombie dropped to the ground.

Henry looked for his next shot, hoping he could save the rest, but as he tried to line up another shot, the woman and boy were each taken down. The boy screamed as a zombie tore out his throat and the woman yelped as a large chunk of her right arm was torn to the bone. Blood shot out and splattered the bed of the pickup as she screamed for her dead son.

Henry ran the few feet so he had a better shot and double-tapped the trigger, killing the ghoul feasting on the boy. Then Jimmy was next to him and a solid blast to the chest of the zombie attacking the woman sent it flying off the pickup to fall onto the road. For a few seconds it was hidden behind the rear fender, but then its head popped up as it struggled to regain its feet. Jimmy was ready and he shot again, blowing the head clean off, the stump its a neck shooting blood a foot in the air to then sputter.

This always fascinated him. If the ghouls were dead, then how the hell could blood pump out when they were shot? He could only assume that though dead, the heart still worked, like the engine of a car with no tires. As long as there was fuel, the engine would work, despite the fact the rest of the car was broken or missing.

The clean-shaven man was on top of the pickup's roof, fending off a female zombie with stringy black hair and a nose ring. He was doing fairly well, but he didn't see the cannie coming up on him from behind. The cannie had decided if he was going to lose his meal ticket, then he could at least make sure the prisoners were dead.

As the cannie moved up and drew a bead on the clean-shaven man, Mary walked up behind the cannie and shot him in the back of the neck, severing the spine from the brain and killing the man instantly. The body pitched forward, dark plasma seeping out to catch what feeble light the pale stars gave off.

As the cannie's body fell like a chopped tree, Mary heard footsteps behind her and she spun around. Before she could fire, the face of the ghoul exploded, the heavy round destroying the decayed visage and dropping the corpse to the pavement.

Mary turned to look into the darkness of the hillside. She waved, knowing Cindy had taken the ghoul down for her.

Henry and Jimmy were doing the same, and working as a team, they finished off the remaining ghouls and Jimmy shot the second to last cannie.

The gunfire eased abruptly and only the screams of the wounded woman and bearded man filled the campsite.

Henry wasn't taking chances though and he raised his left index finger to his lips to tell Mary and Jimmy to be quiet. Both did as they were told and they stood together, eyes searching the darkness for signs of movement.

They all knew if any zombies were still mobile, they would attack without stealth and the cannies wouldn't hold back either.

Both enemies were like Viking warriors and would come at you without fear.

At first there was no sound but the cries of the wounded, then footsteps carried to their ears, the sound of soles slapping cement.

Henry was the first to spot the escaping cannie. He was nothing but a dark shadow amongst other shadows, but he quickly lined up a target and fired, shooting the cannie in the back.

Even in the gloom of the night, Henry saw the shape pitch forward, the momentum of the running man accelerated by the punch to the back as the round slid between bone and found the cannie's heart. Like a clumsy young boy who didn't run well, the cannie plopped face first onto the road, the gravel giving the face a case of road rash as the corpse slid to a stop.

Henry watched the prone shape for a few seconds, and when it didn't move, he was satisfied the cannie was dead.

"That's all of them," Henry said. "Anyone hurt?"

Jimmy shook his head. "I'm good, Mary. How 'bout you?"

"I'm fine," she said. She leaned down next to the crying girl to see how she was. "How are you, honey, are you okay? What's your name?"

The girl's crying slowed slightly and she managed to tell Mary her name.

It was Isabelle.

"Well, hi there, Isabelle," Henry said. "Are you hurt anywhere?"

Isabelle held up her right arm, to show Mary and Henry the bite mark on her arm. The distinct imprint of teeth couldn't be ignored.

Jimmy stepped up and grabbed the girl's arm, staring at the bite mark in the dark shadows.

"Oh, shit, you've got to be kidding, Mary. We did all this for nothing?"

Mary was about to toss a retort at him when more cries of pain came from the pickup truck.

"Mommy!" Isabelle called out and broke from Mary's grip to run to the vehicle.

"No, wait, it's not safe yet!" Mary called after her, then with a glance to Henry and Jimmy, she followed the girl.

Henry looked around the camp, and at the bodies littering the road.

"Mary's right." He turned to Jimmy. "You go do a recce, make sure there's no more surprises. Then circle around and pick up Cindy, Sue and Raven."

"You mean carry her, right?" Jimmy asked, his back still hurting from before.

"Hey, she's your girlfriend," he joked.

"Ha, ha," Jimmy replied as he turned and faded into the outer darkness, his shotgun leading the way. If there were any more ghouls or cannies still around, he had a present for them, wrapped in lead.

Henry followed Mary to the pickup truck to see if he could help.

When he got there, he didn't like what he found.

Isabelle had crawled into the rear bed and was staring at what was left of her family.

The bearded man's right calve was a bloody mess of torn flesh and the ripped material from his pant leg. His hands were on the wound, trying to staunch the blood but spurts of crimson seeped between his fingers.

As Henry drew closer, the man looked up, fear in his eyes, thinking Henry was another zombie, but when he saw Henry wasn't dead or a cannie, he relaxed slightly.

Next to him, his wife was in a world of agony no human should ever know. On top of a gaping two inch hole in her right arm that squirted blood with each beat of her heart, she was leaning down over the still form of her son, who had half his throat ripped out.

The blood on the boy had slowed to a dull trickle, the small blue eyes open but staring at nothing. The boy's mouth was in the shape of an O, as if he couldn't understand how this could happen to him.

After all, children didn't die.

Henry knew if the boy was bit he would die soon, and even now the infection was coursing through his small body. Once dead, the boy would return as one of the walking dead.

Isabelle was crying again and the bearded man, her father, reached out and pulled her close with his left hand.

"It's okay, honey, we're okay, see? We'll get through this, you'll see," the man said softly as he winced in pain from his wound.

"No, it's not okay," Henry said blandly as he eyed the remaining three family members and the clean-shaven man sitting on the roof of the pickup.

The man only watched the tableaux playing out, as if it was a play put on for his entertainment.

Knowing what had to be done, Henry raised his gun.

Chapter 3

"You've all been bit," Henry said. "You know what that means." He gestured to the corpse of the boy. "Even him. If he doesn't get destroyed he's going to get up again and try to kill you." He hesitated then. "But by the looks of you people, I don't think that's gonna matter too much."

"Henry, don't say that," Mary chided as she stood by his side. He turned and cast her a grim look. Her face was lost in the deep shadows of the night, the starlight now blocked by clouds.

"Why, Mary? We can dance around it all night, but it is what it is. Us ignoring it isn't gonna change it one bit." He pointed to Isabelle. "Even she's gonna change. As bad as that sounds."

"I know that, Henry, but..." Mary began.

"But nothing," Henry said coldly. "We can either help them on their way or let them turn and go off and kill more innocents." His gaze bore into hers. "Do you want that, Mary? Do you want more people to die because we couldn't do what had to be done?"

"No, of course not," she said, knowing he spoke the truth.

All the while they talked, the woman wailed for her lost son. Isabelle was crying and the man sobbed, though he tried to be strong for his family.

There was so much ambient noise; neither Mary nor Henry noticed another ghoul crawling up to Henry from underneath the pickup truck. Half its body was gone, only the upper torso remaining. Gunshot residue adorned the bottom half where weapon's fire had sheared the legs from the body. A few dried-out husks of entrails dragged behind it, every now and then a useless organ plopping onto the road like a half full Glad bag of pudding leftover from a picnic.

The bifurcated ghoul dragged itself along until it was within a foot of Henry's left leg. The dry, cracked lips opened wide, the yellow and brown teeth within preparing to taste the warm flesh of the living, when a boot came down on its head and smashed it flat, the desiccated skull cracking like an egg, brains seeping out the sides.

Jimmy looked up into Henry's eyes as the older man glanced down at the crushed head.

"Gettin' lazy in your old age, old man," Jimmy quipped as he let Cindy hop to the end of the pickup. "I think that one was gonna getcha."

Henry frowned deeply, but realized Jimmy was correct, though the probability the ghoul could have sank its teeth past the heavy material of his jeans was iffy, but still, he shouldn't have let the zombie get so close. That settled it for him. He was dancing around what needed to be done, and talking about it wasn't going to change the end result.

Sue and Raven moved up behind him, neither speaking, sensing something heavy was going down.

Cocking his Glock, Henry aimed it at the woman first to do what needed to be done. "Enough of this shit, it has to be done. These aren't my rules, goddammit; they're the world's rules," he said. "You get bit, you get dead, simple as that." The muzzle was a few feet from the woman's head, who shrank back in fear, her dead son now forgotten as she realized her own life was about to be extinguished. "I'm truly sorry to have to do this," Henry said through gritted teeth.

"No, wait, wait a second, please!" This came from the bearded man who jumped in front of his wife. Henry found that ironic, as if by blocking his wife Henry wouldn't shoot. Didn't the man know he was next? Henry could just shoot him first, then the wife.

But something in the man's face halted Henry from squeezing the trigger.

"What? Shit, you're only making this tougher. I don't want to do this, I *have* to do this." Behind Henry, the others stood silent. As the leader of their group, Henry had done many things himself to spare the others hardship or stains on their conscience. All of them knew this was one of those times.

Mary had tears in her eyes as she stared at the shivering form of Isabelle, who didn't understand what was happening. She couldn't imagine how even Henry, with his pragmatic ways, could shoot that beautiful little girl in the head. She knew when it was the girl's time she would have to look away, not wanting to carry that image with her.

"Then don't! Let me do it!" The bearded man's face took on one of absolute pain. "I understand what you're talking about, damn you, and I know you're right," the man said. "I don't want my family walkin' around like one of those damn things. My son, my daughter...never. But let me do it. Let us have a few minutes to say goodbye, to make our peace." His voice cracked with the emotion of what he was saying.

Jimmy stepped up to Henry. "We could give him one of the cannie's guns, Henry. Let him do it. Shit, it is his family after all."

"And you think you can do it? Kill your own family? It's got to be in the head. You know that, right?" Henry said coldly.

The man scowled. "I'm not a fuckin' idiot, asshole, I know what the hell to do," he snapped. Henry let the man's outburst slide, knowing the pain he must be feeling.

"I didn't say you were stupid, friend, but it needs to be done right. And then when you're through, you have to eat a bullet, too."

The man shook his head, tears flying to the sides. "I don't care. Without my family I'd rather be dead anyway. Just give me a fucking gun and leave me to do what I have to."

"Daddy, what's the man talking about? What do you have to do?" Isabelle hugged her daddy, not understanding anything.

"Hush, honey, grownups are talking," he said as he tried to control himself. But his lips trembled and tears poured down his cheeks like two rivers.

Mary was crying to the point she had to walk away, Cindy hobbling after her with Sue assisting. The three women stopped at the front bumper of the pickup and Mary wept while Cindy rubbed her back and Sue stood beside them for support.

On the roof of the truck, the clean-faced man watched it all, immobile, as did Raven, who stood a few feet behind Henry, her black hair making her a ghost in the darkness.

"Let the guy have this, Henry, shoot, it's the least we can do," Jimmy said.

Henry bit his lower lip as his finger caressed the trigger of the Glock; it was still aimed at the man. Finally, he lowered it and looked to Jimmy.

"Fine, go find him a gun. It needs at least four rounds minimum. One for each of them."

Jimmy nodded and moved off into the darkness. The cannies' bodies were spread out, the weapons by their sides, as Jimmy hunted for the one that would do the job. As he moved through the corpses, he came upon a cannie that wasn't quite dead yet. With barely a thought, as if he was stepping on an ant, Jimmy pulled his Bowie knife and sliced the cannie's throat, finishing the job.

Blood shot onto the road as the cannie died for good this time. Jimmy continued on, searching for weapons. He gathered what he could find, knowing the guns could be used as barter in the next town the companions came across. A few weren't worth keeping. They were worn, unmaintained pieces of junk and he tossed them to the roadside. They were the kind of gun where the chances of it going off in you face compared to shooting your attackers were about the same. But he still found four good firearms, including a rifle and a .45 automatic with half a clip. After searching a few more cannies, he also found some more ammunition for the guns, and a small bag with assorted calibers that didn't fit any of the firearms on display. Jimmy figured they were used as currency if the cannies managed to get into a town. As long as they kept their teeth hidden, they could move about to buy supplies and food. Even cannies knew they couldn't live on just human flesh, they needed vegetables and other forms of nutrients, but their main diet was still Long Pig.

Jimmy returned to the rear bed of the pickup truck to see the clean-shaven man was now on the road, standing next to Henry and Raven. In the pickup bed, the three remaining family members huddled together as the woman caressed Isabelle's temple and cried into her hair. The bearded man's visage as well as the woman's was one of absolute anguish.

"Jimmy, meet, Lyle," Henry said, introducing the clean-shaven man. "He's clean, no bites anywhere."

"Hi there, glad to see you made it through unharmed," Jimmy said as he handed Henry the guns. "These are the best of the lot, the others are junk."

"Yeah, no shit," Lyle replied but then held his tongue. He didn't want Henry to change his mind for some reason and add him in with the family. Lyle watched warily as Henry and Jimmy discussed the gun the bearded man was going to use to kill his family. As he did this, he studied Henry and Jimmy, took in their postures, their weapons.

Military trained, Lyle knew fellow warriors when he saw them. He figured Henry and his group were mercenaries. They had to be the way they took out the cannie convoy like a well-drilled unit.

"You see something interesting, pal?" Henry asked of Lyle.

Lyle realized he was looking a little too intently and had been caught. Quickly shaking his head, he decided in sticking as close to the truth as possible.

"Oh, I ah, I was just admiring your weapons, that's all. I was thinking you guys must be mercies, am I right?"

Henry gave no sign the man was right or wrong.

"Think what you want, I really don't care. Why the hell does it matter?" Henry growled.

"Oh, shit, man, it doesn't, I was just, you know..."

"Whatever," Henry added. "Just stand there and be quiet. Once this is over with we'll deal with you."

"Fine, fine, it's cool, I get it. I owe you for saving my ass," Lyle said, raising his hands before him in a gesture of surrender

"Yeah, you do, so don't try anything. Hear me?" Henry's tone was cold.

"Yeah, man, I got it, I'm not moving. I'll stay right here till you tell me to do something else."

Henry stared at Lyle for three seconds, making sure the man was on the level and not bullshitting him, then he went back to talking to Jimmy.

Lyle looked to the front of the pickup to see Mary, Sue and Cindy waiting quietly. Mary was now more composed but her eyes were red. Even in the shadows of the night, Lyle could see this.

"Hey, Mary, Sue and Cindy!" Henry called out.

"What, Henry," Mary replied.

"Check out that car and see if we can take it with us. It's worth a lot in trade in the next town."

Mary nodded and said okay, and with Cindy hobbling beside her as well as Sue, the three women went to check out the Datsun to see if they could take it with them along with the pickup truck.

Henry looked at Raven. "Want to make yourself useful?"

She nodded yes.

"Go check through the bodies and see what you can find. Hell, even a cigarette lighter is worth something in trade."

She nodded and turned to go searching.

"And be careful," he called after her like a worried father.

She waved that she would and was soon lost in the night.

Henry turned to Jimmy, gesturing to a .45 automatic in his hand.

"How's that one, Jimmy? Does it have bullets?"

"Yeah, it's got a half clip," Jimmy replied, handing the gun to Henry.

Henry took it and popped out the clip. On the side of the clip was a hollow line where he could see how many rounds were still inside.

"Jimmy, go check out the pickup truck; make sure it's drivable."

"Okay, got it," Jimmy replied and jogged away, still carrying the extra firearms.

When Henry was through inspecting the clip, and satisfied there was more than enough to do the job, he handed the .45 to the bearded man, who took it with a shaky grip.

"You got a name, friend?" Henry asked.

The bearded man nodded. "Harrison, John Harrison, and this is my wife, Susan. And you already know my daughter, Isabelle." His voice broke as he said the next words. "And that was my son, Jason."

"Yeah, I'm real sorry about that, John." Henry said and shrugged. "There's not much more to say, is there?"

John shook his head slowly, knowing Henry spoke the truth.

Mary came back to them, Cindy waiting by the end of the pickup with Sue. Her ankle was hurting a lot and she didn't want to move if she didn't have to.

Henry turned to Mary as she approached. "Well, what's the verdict?"

Mary shook her head. "The car's trashed, Henry. It's got two flat tires and it looks like it took at least three rounds to the engine."

"Damn it, would have been nice to have two vehicles. Oh well, hopefully the pickup didn't take any unnecessary lead."

As if in reply to his answer, Jimmy started the engine of the pickup, blue-black smoke spitting out the exhaust to be lost in the darkness. He turned on the headlights, the parking lights now bathing Henry in a red glow as the headlights illuminate the bodies spread across the road.

Henry nodded. "Good, at least something's gone right tonight." He turned back to John. "You need to hop out of there, John, I need this pickup." His tone said this wasn't a request. But then Henry's voice softened a little. "I'll help you with your son."

John said nothing, his voice locked in his throat. He climbed down onto the ground, and with Henry's help, they carefully carried his son's body to the edge of the road. After that his wife was next. She had said nothing since being bitten and seeing her son killed. As Henry helped her down to the road, he saw her eyes were glazed and her mouth was slack. It looked to him like she was dead already; she just didn't know it yet.

Isabelle was next and that was the hardest for Henry. He picked her up under her arms, feeling how light she was, and set her down onto the road. John was standing there, the gun now behind his back to keep it hidden.

"Where are we going now, Daddy?" Isabelle asked sweetly. "Are we going with them? I like Mary, she's nice. She saved me from the bad men and the monsters."

John began to cry again, but he managed to hold it together for just a little longer.

"No, honey, we're going to stay here for a while. Say goodbye to the nice people, they're leaving now."

"Oh, okay," Isabelle said and turned to Mary who had walked up behind her. "Bye, Mary, thanks for saving me. My arm hurts, though."

Mary had tears in her eyes as she hugged the little girl.

"Why are you crying, Mary? Is it because of what happened to my brother? I'm sad, too. Daddy says people die all the time now and we have to be brave."

Mary nodded, wiped her nose on her sleeve, and gave the girl her best smile.

"He's right, Isabelle, and you're the bravest little girl I've ever met. You take care of your Mom and Dad now, okay?" Mary said, her voice on the verge of cracking.

"I will. Mommy's sad because of Jason, so I'm gonna go give her a hug."

She walked away then, moving through the darkness as she headed for her mother. As she passed the rear taillights of the pickup, her face was cast in crimson. Mary saw this and felt her heart break a little more, knowing what was going to happen to that little girl.

John let out a few choked sobs, not able to contain himself.

Jimmy walked up to them, having turned off the engine to save gas, and he shook his head. "Christ, this sucks big-time."

No one replied.

John's wound was bleeding heavily, leaving a dark trail on the road, but the man ignored it. He knew he would be dead long before he bled out so what was the point in treating the wound?

Henry moved closer to John, his face downcast. He held out his right hand for John to shake. "I'm so sorry for you, John. I can't even begin to tell you how much. We all are."

John nodded in reply, his lower lip trembling. Henry could see the man was about to lose it. Henry decided to get the others away so they didn't have to see the man in this condition.

Raven popped back up with a handful of items. Nothing special but a few would be worth something in trade. Without asking, she dropped them in the rear of the pickup.

"Okay," Henry said to the others. "We're headin' out. Get our stuff loaded, get Cindy inside the cab, and then get ready. I just need to talk to John for another second."

Mary and Jimmy said okay and began to move about, grabbing their gear, which Jimmy had brought down with Cindy from the hillside. Cindy did what she could but with her bad ankle it wasn't much and Sue took up her slack, carrying what Cindy needed. Henry turned to Lyle, forgetting the man was still there, as he'd been so quiet. "You coming with us?"

"Yeah that would be great, thanks," Lyle responded.

"Okay, then go see Jimmy and see what help he needs. Everyone pulls their weight if they travel with us."

"Got it, thanks, Henry," Lyle said and walked away. A second later, Jimmy was directing the man on what he wanted him to do.

Henry turned back to John.

"Look, this is what's going to happen next. I'm getting in that truck with my people and we're gonna drive down the road a bit. Then I'm gonna park and wait. If I don't hear four shots, I'm coming back to do what I should have done now. I just want you to be totally clear on this. It might not seem like it, John, but I'm doing you a favor here."

"No, Henry, I get it, I do. Thank you again," John said, his voice on the verge of slipping into mindless shrieks of sorrow and pain.

"Okay, don't take too long either, I want to get moving. With all the gunshots fired off in the last few minutes, any deader in a half mile radius is gonna be on this place shortly. So even if you decided not to go through with it and I left you here, you'd only end up getting ripped apart when they show up."

"Yeah, Henry, I got it, I understand. Me and my family are fucked anyway you cut it."

"Yeah, John, 'fraid so." Henry glanced at the little girl who was hugging her catatonic mother. "I'd do your daughter first. That way she doesn't see it coming. Just have her look away at a tree or something and then, you know, in the back of the head. She'll never feel a thing."

John finally snapped and he pulled the gun from his back and tried to aim it at Henry, spittle flying from his mouth. But Henry was ready. He brought his arm up and forced John's arm up into the air, then he kicked out with his right foot, breaking John's knee.

The man screamed as he fell to the road, and Henry pulled the gun from his hand.

"How can you be so cold? How can you make me do this to my family! You can't be this heartless!" John screamed.

Henry turned to see Jimmy moving towards him and he raised his hand to stop him. "I got this, Jimmy, get in the truck, we're leaving in a second." He saw Isabelle watching, her eyes wide with fear as her father wailed and cried and Henry nodded to her. "It's fine, honey, me and your daddy are just talking. He'll be over there with you in a second."

Isabelle nodded though her face was still a mask of worry.

Henry reached down and picked John up, the wounded man crying out in pain. In the wan light from the stars, the white of bone could be seen piercing the man's pant leg. Even if he was going to live, his leg was now ruined forever.

"I'll give you a pass on that one 'cause I can't imagine what you're going through right now," Henry hissed in John's ear. "But trust me on this. You try anything like that again, and I'll kill you myself, then I'll shoot your wife and daughter, as distasteful as that is. Now, goddammit, you're the man in their lives. Do this one last thing to spare them any more pain. It's your duty as a father and a husband." John was sobbing now, heavily, and Henry shook the man hard. "John, snap out of it, man. Do you hear what I'm telling you?"

Through sniffles and tears, John nodded. "Yes, yes, I hear you, I'm sorry I lost it. I just want someone to blame, is all. I know this isn't your doing."

"Well then blame God, this is all his screwed up work. I don't know what the hell we did as a species to piss him off but he sure as hell is angry with us," Henry replied. "Come on, let me help you to your family."

Henry slung an arm under John's right arm pit and helped the man hobble to the shoulder of the road where Isabelle was waiting for him. She went out and took his hand, as if her small frame could support him.

"Daddy, Mommy's hurt too and I have a boo-boo. Are you gonna help us?"

Through cracked sobs, John nodded. "Yes, honey, in a few minutes I promise there will be no more pain."

"Why are you crying, Daddy? Are you sad for Jason?"

"Yes, I am, now go sit down next to Mommy for me, please."

She did as she was told and John looked over to Henry.

"Happy?"

"No, John, I'm not, but it has to be done." Henry handed him the .45 again.

"Here, now be strong and do this one last thing for them."

Henry moved away, but his hand never left his Glock as he walked backwards from John. He wasn't going to take any chances that the man might still try something crazy. The warrior in him yelled at him for being so sentimental, so foolhardy, but the man he once was, the moral, compassionate and merciful man knew this was the right thing to do.

When Henry reached the pickup truck, he climbed into the back with Lyle, Sue and Mary. Cindy was in the cab with Jimmy and Raven.

"Okay, Jimmy, get going. We're done here, but pull over and stop when I tell you to, okay?" Henry called.

"Sure, old man, not a problem."

Jimmy put the transmission into drive and pulled around the Datsun, the front tires driving over bodies like they were piles of dirt. In the rear bed, Henry and the others had to hold on tight or risk being thrown off the back.

Mary stared at Henry and he only nodded to her. "Yeah, Mary, I know it stinks, but that's life."

"Or death," she whispered.

"Yeah, honey, or death."

They drove for less than a minute and Henry had Jimmy pull over.

"So what are we waiting here for?" Jimmy asked.

"Just wait, you'll see," Henry said softly, only the ticking engine breaking the sounds of the night. The sky was clear; most of the clouds having broken up and the starlight was now stronger, allowing each of the companions to see each other. Lyle, being the outsider, said nothing, merely watching his saviors silently.

The pickup sat on the side of the road for another five minutes and Henry was about to make Jimmy turn around and head back, when the first gunshot echoed down the road and into the night sky.

"That was Isabelle," Henry said softly, Mary immediately breaking into tears.

More than a minute passed without another shot and Henry was once again ready to make Jimmy turn around when there was another shot, followed by another.

"That was the wife and the dead son, so he doesn't come back," Henry said. "One more and we're good."

Three more minutes ticked by, seeming like forever as each of the companions stared at the other, knowing what was happening down the road. A wail of agony and loss drifted to them in the night air, and it was the unmistakable voice of John, perhaps going mad with having to kill his family.

"Henry I..." Mary began, and then she jumped slightly when one last shot rolled across the road.

"And that's John eating a bullet," Henry said coldly.

Jimmy swiveled around and stuck his head out the window so he could see Henry. "What about the .45? Aren't we gonna go back for it?"

Henry shook his head. "Nah, leave it, we got enough extras for trading, let that one stay with the dead." He pointed into the darkness of the road ahead. "Get goin', Jimmy, let's see what's down this road."

Jimmy nodded, slid back into the cab, and drove onward.

Mary slid over to Henry who took her in his arms, holding her tightly. He reached his free hand out for Sue who took it, the two holding hands now.

"She was a beautiful little girl, wasn't she, Henry? What kind of God would let her die like that?" Mary asked.

"An angry one," Henry said softly. He got comfortable as the pickup drove on, the headlights cutting through the night, banishing the darkness, even if it was just for a few moments in time.

Chapter 4

For the next hour, the pickup truck drove through the back roads, meandering like a farmer out for a Sunday drive. Everyone was subdued after what had happened back at the cannie camp, and Mary was hit the hardest.

She still found it difficult to believe little Isabelle was dead, shot in the head by her father.

Lyle was the only one to do the talking really. As Henry, Sue and Mary listened, Lyle filled them in on how he had been caught by the cannies and how he had been as sure as anything in this world that he was going to end up in a stew pot.

For most of his tale, Henry barely listened, understanding the man was just happy to be alive, that is, until Lyle mentioned where he was from.

"So you're saying your town is how big?" Henry asked, still shocked at the number Lyle had said.

"About a thousand of us. Why, is that a lot?" Lyle asked, not getting where Henry was going with his question.

"Yeah, that's a lot of people in one place. I'd have to say that's the biggest settlement we've come across since the Groton Naval Base in Connecticut, wouldn't you say, Mary?"

She nodded. "Yes, sounds right. There were a lot of people there, too. From what Raddack said at least a thousand, maybe more. They were all spread out through the base."

"I thought the military wasn't running anymore," Lyle said. "You were at a functioning naval base?"

Henry shook his head, then held on tight as the pickup went over a nasty pothole. "No it wasn't functioning for real, well, not by the military. Look, it's a long story and not worth going into. But up to a few months ago there were people living at the naval base. When we left it was being overrun by the dead." He waved his right hand to get Lyle back on track. "So, your town, are strangers welcome there?"

"You mean like you guys? Hell, yeah, especially after I tell them what you did to save my ass from gettin' eaten."

"So we can take you there and we'll be welcomed, too?" Mary inquired.

"Shit, yeah, I promise you that," Lyle said merrily. "Mayor Bigelow is a good man. He's fair and runs a tight ship. He was the man who got us organized and had the great wall built so the dead couldn't get in. He sectioned off some parts of the town to grow crops and raise livestock, not to mention he has dances and activities every weekend so the townspeople would have something to look forward to, you know, to take their mind off what's happened to the world. Yes, sir, things are pretty damn good in Cement City."

"Cement City? That's a weird name for a town," Mary said, perking up a little now that she had something to take her mind off things.

"Yeah, I suppose it is, but I've never given it much thought, really. You see, I've lived there all my life. Do you guys want to know how we got that name?"

Henry, Sue and Mary shrugged. They were a captive audience and any story was fine to pass the time.

Lyle rubbed his hands together, warming up to telling the history of his home town.

"Well, it's not really that great a story but back in 1901, a man by the name of William Cowhan built a cement plant on the south side of town. The man was so powerful he pretty much owned the town, and he was able to get the name changed to Cement City. The plant is nothing but ruins now, mostly a hangout for teenagers, but it's still there. It's a great place to bring a girl as it's on the shore of Goose Lake, and from there you can see the Irish Hills. In the summer, when the sun sets, it's absolutely fantastic."

"Sounds like maybe you've been there a few times with a date?" Mary smiled. Now that she had a chance to really look at Lyle with the light from the stars, she realized he was quite handsome, with a strong jaw and deep brown eyes. He seemed to smile at any little thing with a pleasant personality. It was at that moment when she realized she was attracted to him and it caught her off guard. For the past two years, she had been so busy running and fighting, any form of a relationship had seemed out of the question. But then, if Cindy and Jimmy could do it, then why couldn't she?

"Yeah, a few times," Lyle replied as he smiled at Mary. "Maybe I could take you there and show you myself when we get there?" His eyes went up with hope.

"That sounds nice, Lyle, I just might take you up on it," Mary said with a grin.

"You will?" Henry asked, surprised.

She moved so she could look at him, though in the dark he was just another shadow, the starlight coming in from behind him.

"Yes, Henry I will. Why, can't I have some fun once in a while?"

"Yes, Henry, can't she?" Sue asked, the women ganging up on him.

"Of course, Mary, you're a big girl, you can do whatever you want," he said, feeling trapped by the two females. He was glad they couldn't see him blush as he was acting like a stern father making sure his daughter didn't do something bad on a date.

"That's right, Henry, I'm a big girl and I can do whatever I want," Mary repeated.

Henry decided he needed a distraction, something to change the subject, and when he looked to the right side of the road, he saw they were coming upon a stream. Figuring this was as good a place as any other to stay for the night, he leaned forward and slapped the roof of the pickup.

"Hey, Jimmy, pull it over to the right side! There's a stream and over there. We can make camp and wash up there, too."

"Sounds good, Henry!" Jimmy replied and immediately the engine began to wind down as the vehicle began to slow. Jimmy bumped over the shoulder of the road and put the pickup between two large trees, almost as if the spot had been waiting for him. The shoulder was overgrown with weeds and shrubs. With man no longer maintaining it, the greenery was growing wild. Already many of the bushes and tree branches were hanging either over or in the road. In a few more years, the vegetation would shrink the road to barely passable and another ten years the road would vanish under a layer of green and moss.

Jimmy turned off the engine and everyone climbed out except for Cindy.

As Henry jumped down off the rear bed, he spotted a shadow in the shape of a human being come out of the woods.

"Heads up, people, we're not alone here," Henry hissed as he drew his Glock, Jimmy and Mary doing the same. Sue move behind Henry and Raven waited by Mary's side, her hands ready to slash if necessary.

"Whoever's there, don't move or I'll blow your damn head off," Henry warned.

None of the companions moved, each standing perfectly still with their weapons drawn and now aimed at the solitary figure.

As the figure stepped forward, a sliver of light pierced the tree tops and exposed the desiccated face of a ghoul. It wasn't a fresh one, with boils of pus leaking from its face and oozing holes in its exposed flesh. Its clothes were tatters, nothing but rags, and flies and maggots were either floating over it or crawling on it.

Immediately everyone relaxed slightly, realizing they weren't being ambushed. It was just a lone zombie that was stumbling about in the underbrush and had been attracted to the sounds of the pickup truck pulling into the area.

Jimmy raised his shotgun, about to blow the ghoul to hell when Henry called to him. "No, Jimmy, don't waste the shell, I got this one. Everyone go set up for the night."

Jimmy, knowing Henry could handle one lone zombie easily, nodded and went to help Cindy out of the cab of the pickup, while Mary and Sue led Lyle away from the vehicle.

"But what about the zombie? Aren't you gonna kill it?" Lyle asked Mary and Sue as they moved away down to the stream.

"Henry's got it; he'll take care of it, Lyle. Trust me, this isn't the first time. He knows what he's doing."

"Watch yourself, old man," Jimmy cautioned as he helped Cindy hobble away, their packs over his free shoulder.

"I'll be with you guys in second, just let me take care of this first," Henry grinned.

Raven was hovering near Henry and he turned to look at her. "What?"

"Want to stay, make sure you don't mess it up."

He chuckled at her. "I think I can handle one deader, Raven. You go back and watch the others' backs, I'll be right along."

She looked like she was going to protest as he pointed at her. He was smiling but his eyes were cold. He was the leader and he wasn't going to argue each time he gave an order. That could get them killed.

"Just go," he said one last time. She shrugged, turned and left, gliding over the ground with the stealth of a cat.

As the companions and Lyle moved away, the zombie stood still. It didn't know what target to go for as there were so many. Its dead mind couldn't calculate very well, and so it stood stock still.

Once everyone had moved through the bushes and trees lining the stream, the ghoul saw only Henry, and with a low moan, it took a step toward the deadlands warrior, arms raised with hands open to grasp and rend.

Henry stood perfectly still, a slight smile creasing his lips as the ghoul stumbled towards him like a newborn taking its first steps.

Five feet, four feet, still Henry didn't move. His hands were at his sides, hovering over his Glock and the handle of his panga.

Three feet and Henry could smell the decay and rot. This zombie was ripe, the maggots crawling in and out of the orifices while flies buzzed over the matted scalp like tiny helicopters waiting for clearance to land.

At two feet Henry could see the dead eyes glaring back at him, the brown and black teeth, coated with layers of dried blood; the shriveled black tongue that lay in the bottom of the mouth like a dead slug.

One foot.

In a blur of movement, Henry reached down, grasped the hilt of his panga, and pulled it free, at the same time sidestepping to the right so he was now on the left side of the ghoul. As the zombie spun to counter the move, Henry brought up the panga and sliced downward, the arc taking the blade through the neck and into the top of the shoulder, shearing off a three inch hunk of flesh as the blade finished its route of death.

For a second, the ghoul stopped moving, the mouth opening and closing slowly. Then the head began to slide off the neck, leaving an angled cut that exposed muscle, tendon and spine. The head toppled to the ground and rolled a few feet as the headless corpse swayed like an aged oak too many years on this earth.

Then, like the same fabled tree, the body toppled over to land in a puff of dust, dark, cold blood seeping out of the jagged neck wound to soak into the soil.

The flies, angered at being disturbed, dissipated for a brief minute, but in seconds they were back to feed on the coagulated plasma soaking into the dirt and making it into a muddy slurry.

Henry leaned forward and wiped his blade clean on the back of the corpse's tattered pants, while smiling to himself. The kill had taken less than thirty seconds. No fanfare, no major battle as he fought for his life.

The truth was, in single numbers, the zombies were nothing but a pain in the ass. It was only when their numbers grew that they were a true threat.

Resheathing his panga when he was sure it was clean, he reached down, grabbed the corpse by its pant legs and dragged it across the road and into the bushes. When he went back, he used his boot to kick the head onto the road, for all purposes looking like a kid playing with a soccer ball.

When he was at the shoulder once more, he gently nudged the head against the decapitated corpse. The milky-white eyes never ceased to roll back and forth in their sockets.

As long as the brain was intact, the head would function, but with no body it was harmless.

With the body disposed of, Henry went back to where he had killed it. He kicked some dirt over the area to hide the blood and then went to join his friends.

The stream looked inviting and he was looking forward to dunking his head in the water, or better yet, perhaps even taking a dip.

Chapter 5

The moon was a thin sliver in the night sky as the seven people stretched out and relaxed under the canopy of stars.

The water was far too cold for swimming but everyone had taken bird baths, the men stripping down to their waists while the women were more modest. Cindy sat on a low boulder at the edge of the stream, her bad ankle now soaking in the cold water. It felt like heaven and the swelling had already gone down by half.

Jimmy, seeing Cindy all alone, went over and sat down beside her. His boots and socks were off and he soaked his feet also, relishing the coolness of the water. A few small fish, not much bigger than the size of his pinky, poked at his feet, their small mouths opening and closing. Neither spoke, Cindy leaning against him, placing her head on his shoulder, as Jimmy wrapped an arm around her, pulling her close.

For all purposes, they looked like two young lovers who had snuck out to the woods on a Friday night to make out.

Henry stretched out on the grass as he stared up at the night sky. Sue was beside him and she was already sleeping. Raven was ten feet away, stretched out and sleeping lightly, and Lyle was a few feet to Henry's right, with Mary on his left.

"You know, it's funny how clear the sky is now," Henry said. "I remember back before everything changed how I could barely see a star from my backyard."

"That's because there was light pollution back then, Henry," Mary informed him as she gazed up into the twinkling sky.

"Huh?" Henry replied.

"Light pollution. Oh, come on, Henry, you never heard of it? It's when there's so many lights lit up on our planet that the ambient glow is so bright it reflects off the atmosphere. Thus we can't see the stars very well. But now, with most of the population walking around as deaders, well, there's not as much light, hardly a fraction I suppose. And there's sure as hell not a lot of electrical lights anymore."

Henry nodded, agreeing with her. "Yeah, that makes sense. Light pollution. So you're saying almost all of the population of the world had to die so I could see the stars again?"

"Unfortunately it seems like that, huh," she replied.

Lyle spoke up, wanting in on the conversation. "I remember astronomers partitioning for stricter rules on the amount of light from cities. They hated it because of the very thing Mary just said. That's why they would build those big telescopes way out in the middle of nowhere."

Mary nodded, agreeing with him. "Hey, yeah, that's right. They built them on mountains, too."

"Bingo," he said, smiling at her. She smiled back and Henry looked at her and then Lyle. He wasn't so old he didn't recognize the look they were throwing at one another. It looked like perhaps Mary was attracted to Lyle.

Henry got to his feet.

"Where're you going?" Mary inquired.

"Nowhere, Mary, I just thought I'd check around the perimeter, make sure there are no more surprises, like that deader we found waiting for us." He grinned slightly. "You kids stay and talk, I'll be back."

Mary nodded and Lyle waved slightly, just a flick of his hand in parting. Henry moved off, his palm on his Glock out of force of habit. As he strolled through the glade alongside the stream, he came upon Jimmy and Cindy. The couple was talking softly and Cindy was smiling. Henry noticed whenever Cindy was talking with Jimmy she was smiling, as Jimmy had that effect on her.

"Hey, guys, I'm gonna go for a walk and check out the area. You kids be good."

"Sure, Henry, not a problem," Jimmy said. He never looked up, only having eyes for Cindy.

As Henry moved off, Jimmy chatted his girl up. He was hoping later, when everyone was bedded down for the night, he could get in a little fun with her.

As he whispered sweet nothings into her ear, he didn't see the water begin to stir just below his feet, the ripples contrary to the current of the stream. The water undulated like a rock had been dropped into it and as he tried to convince Cindy it would be okay if they fooled around later, a waterlogged and desiccated hand slowly slid out of the surface of the stream.

The fingernails on the hand were missing, red and black sores replacing where they'd been. The skin was peeling in places, the dark tendons and muscle visible. The skin on the hand was all but wrinkled to the point of flaking off and with each inch of it rising out the water, the arm connected to it was exposed.

The zombie had crawled for miles in the stream, never feeling the need to leave the cool water, but now it had spotted Jimmy and Cindy through the rippling current and it was rising to feed.

Jimmy, oblivious of an attack from the stream, continued chatting with Cindy and he only stopped when he felt the cold grasp of the wrinkled hand wrap around his left ankle.

"What the fu…?" was all he managed to utter before the hand pulled back and he was sliding off the boulder to plummet into the stream. He had time to hear Cindy scream once in surprise and shock before he was pulled under the surface, his ears filling with water.

He managed to take a quick gasp of air before his head went under and now his eyes blinked at the pale face of death before him. The ghoul's face was all but missing, the nose long gone to be replaced by a gaping hole. The eyes were sunken in and one looked like it was about to pop out, while the ears had rotted and floated away long ago. The skull-like visage still had teeth and they clacked under the water, Jimmy hearing it like someone was clapping erasers together.

The other hand of the ghoul reached out and grabbed his arm and with him off balance, Jimmy found he was helpless to stop the ghoul from taking a bite out of him.

As the teeth went for his cheek, he managed to get his right hand under the rotting chin and push it away. His hand sank a quarter inch into the putrid flesh and only the water washing it away from his touch allowed him to handle the sensation. It was like sticking his hand into cold mud.

As the ghoul clacked its teeth and tried to take a chunk out of him, Jimmy rolled around on the floor of the stream. He began to move with the current, the ghoul and he locked in a death grip, and he floated away from Cindy and the boulder. Muffled yells came to his ears as Cindy cried out to the others.

But Jimmy knew they would never be able to save him in time. This was up to him. Live or die, he would be the one to choose his fate.

As he bounced off the streambed, rocks sliced into his back, only his heavy shirt saving him from severe wounds. The ghoul never ceased its attack, teeth constantly trying to feed on his flesh as the gnarled hands flailed out, seeking an eye or his mouth.

No sooner did the zombie try this then an index finger slipped between Jimmy's lips. Instinctively Jimmy bit down, severing the digit from the hand as a brown liquid seeped from the jagged wound at the nub of the digit. He spit out the finger and watched it float away, and when he opened his mouth, the water washed away the foul taste of the finger. He never swallowed and in seconds his mouth was clean and he thanked the gods for small favors.

The ghoul wrapped its hand with all the fingers into Jimmy's hair and yanked back, causing him to cry out. Water slid into his airway and he began to choke. Punching the ghoul in the face, Jimmy managed to free himself of its grasp and he pushed up with his upper body, his face clearing the surface for a second. Sucking in air and water, he was pulled back down as the zombie renewed its attack.

Lightheaded, his vision blurry, Jimmy still felt revived from the little air he managed to suck into his laboring lungs.

This gave him the energy he needed to reach down to his hip and find his Bowie knife. For a panicked moment, he couldn't find it and his trip hammering heart skipped another beat as his hand felt around with no result, but then his fingers touched the hilt and he pulled it free of its sheath. As the zombie groaned and moaned in the water, not needing to breathe, Jimmy brought the blade around in a wide arc and jammed the nine inch blade into to the ghoul's left ear. If he had down this above the water's surface, the blow would have plunged the knife in with great force, but the water slowed his blow. Still, the tip slid into the zombie's ear canal.

Jimmy pushed harder, finishing the job, and the blade bit deep, slicing into the zombie's brain. Jimmy twisted the knife hard to the left, slicing the brain into pieces, and the zombie twitched and spasmed as whatever had animated it a few years ago now drained away.

Feeling the corpse go limp, Jimmy kicked it off him and it tumbled away with the current.

No sooner did he do this then he felt another hand reach down from above and grab him by his shirt collar. As he was pulled out of the water, the nine inch blade was already coming around to strike at the new foe when he heard Henry's voice cut through the haze of his oxygen-deprived mind.

"Whoa, easy there, Jimmy, it's me!" Henry yelled as he dodged the sweeping blow of the Bowie knife. Jimmy pulled his blow at the last second and the blade missed Henry by inches.

"Oh, shit," Jimmy sputtered. "I thought you were another one of them, Henry," he gasped as he was pulled onto dry land to lie on the ground like a landed fish.

Turning his head to the side, he saw the boulder and Cindy still standing on it only fifty feet away. It seemed like he had gone further when he was under the water, but he guessed his sense of distance was knocked askew.

Mary, Sue and Lyle were there with Henry and Lyle leaned down to help him up.

"Easy there, buddy, you had yourself quite a dunking."

Jimmy was on his feet but leaning over with his hands on his knees, the Bowie knife still clutched in his hand.

Lyle shook his head in amazement. "Jesus Christ, that was the most unbelievable thing I've ever seen. I didn't know they could get you from in the water. That's something new altogether."

Henry nodded, agreeing with him. "It happened to us before when we were swimming in a lake, but I didn't think the stream would be an issue with the current and all. They don't need to breathe and they can just walk around in the bottom of a lake or river until some poor soul wanders by. Then all they have to do is reach up and grab you. Christ, even rivers and streams are danger-ous.”

“Jimmy! You okay?” Cindy called out from where she stood. She couldn’t run thanks to her bad ankle, and her face was creased with concern. Behind her, Raven appeared, looking on with mild concern.

“I’m fine, babe, piece of cake,” Jimmy called back, but he glanced at Henry and sighed, the gesture telling Henry that was the farthest thing from the truth.

Henry grinned wanly. “Well, it’s good to see you’re okay, and hey, look at the bright side to all of this.”

“Bright side? Old man, what could possibly be the bright side to getting attacked by a deader and pulled into the stream?”

Henry shrugged. “Well, at least now you don’t need a bath.”

Chapter 6

The darkness was complete over the stream and makeshift campsite. A few night birds called to one another in the trees and a cricket here and there played a symphony of nature.

Mary leaned against a large tree and sighed, enjoying the solitude of being on watch.

Behind her, near the pickup truck, the others slept restlessly.

Low hanging branches were cut from trees to then be spread around the campsite like a loose, rough fence. It wasn't perfect, but it would alert Mary or one of the others if something or someone tried to get into the camp while they slept.

As Mary let her gaze drift over the shapes of the boulders near the stream and the trees, her imagination began to get the better of her. A tree to her right looked a lot like a zombie, with its low branches, which seemed to be arms. The trunk was thinner in the middle and it gave it the appearance of a waist, the wide hips making the figure seem almost seductive.

Gripping her .38 tighter, she spun at the sound of a twig snapping behind her.

She knew there was more than an hour before Henry would take her place on watch, so her instincts were on full alert. With the barrel of the weapon leading the way, she found her self looking at the frightened face of Lyle, who was now standing with his arms to his sides as he waited to feel the kiss of death.

"Wait, don't shoot, it's just me," he said as he stared at the muzzle of the gun. "I just wanted to talk to you."

Mary lowered the gun and let out the breath she was holding. "Then you shouldn't go around sneaking up on people in the middle of the woods like that. It's a good way to get yourself shot."

He nodded. "I hear ya, but I didn't want to call out for obvious reasons." He gestured to the sleeping forms in the cab and rear bed of the pickup.

She studied his face in the shadows, the strong chin, the clean face that now had just the hint of stubble, and she smiled. "Okay, I'll let you off with a warning this time, but next time…"

He stepped closer to her. "There won't be a next time, Officer, I promise."

She chuckled, and as she did, she almost wanted to slap herself. The chuckle was that of a school girl who was finally getting to talk to the handsome boy she had a crush on.

Lyle moved so close to her she could smell his scent and it awakened feelings in her she'd been keeping hidden for almost two years. Since the outbreak she had been celibate. Not by choice, but by the simple fact there had been no time to meet someone and cultivate a relationship. But she had also never met someone like Lyle before who seemed to connect with her on a subconscious level. She had to wonder if this was what was meant by love at first sight, but she knew that was ridiculous. Still, in a small way she knew that if she had the chance, she wanted to jump this man's bones. She felt silly for thinking that as it was so far removed from who she was. A one night stand would have been something she wouldn't have done in her wildest dreams, but then her world wasn't the same anymore and neither was she.

The old morals of humanity were a thing of the past, and most survivors knew to grab pleasures in life whenever they could, for the next minute could be death to themselves or a friend.

"I like your laugh," he said, pulling her from her reverie.

She smiled bashfully, thankful for the darkness. "Thanks, I've had it all my life."

"So, where are you from, you know, originally?" Lyle asked as he moved closer still. He was only a few inches away from her and she could smell his breath when he talked. It smelled like beef jerky, and for some reason it was the most sensual odor in the world to her right then.

"Uhm, California was where I was born, but then I moved to the Midwest. My parents are, well, I pray they are, still back in California, but the odds of them…"

"Yes, Mary, I know what you mean. It's hard not knowing. At least if you knew they were dead you could accept it, but to not know, perhaps never know. Well, I assume it's a lot like how a parent feels when a child is abducted and never found. It's the wondering that would drive you mad in the end." He paused and she said nothing so he continued. "My folks and little sister are from South Carolina but I don't know about them either. Though I have to figure they're dead. I heard my city got hit pretty bad when the rains first fell."

Mary could hear the angst in his voice and as a person who had an incredible amount of compassion for others, she reached out and took his right hand in comfort.

"I know, Lyle, I'm so sorry for you."

"Yeah, well, I guess we're all in the same boat here, right?"

She nodded, the gesture barely discernable in the shadows.

"Sure we are. Henry lost his wife, Cindy her parents and brother, and Jimmy lost his parents. There's more people, too, of course but those were the closest to them. I suppose everyone's lost something or someone. But we've got to carry on, right?"

"I guess so," he replied. "Though sometimes I have to wonder what's the point."

"The point?"

"Uh-huh," he said. "Why keep fighting when there's no way to win. Mary, how can you fight something that's already dead? Sooner or later they're gonna win, they have to, it's fate."

"Well, Lyle, I try not to think like that and neither does Henry or any of the others. That's why we'll win in the end, because we won't give up."

"I hear ya, Mary, but there's just one problem with that formula."

"And that is?"

"The dead won't give up either."

She didn't reply this time, his words cutting to the heart of the matter. He had a point, but what else was there to do? Just give up and die? Or become one of them?

No, Mary knew as long as Henry and the others were with her she would continue to fight, even if at times she didn't know what she was fighting for.

"Hey, enough of this depressing talk, why don't we change the subject," he suggested. She caught a hint of a smile in the darkness from him and it made her heart skip a beat.

"Okay, you pick a topic," she said.

And he did, deciding to tell her more about his town, Cement City, and as he talked, Mary listened attentively, though one ear was always alert for signs of danger.

But the woods along the stream were silent, the companions safe, so she leaned back against the tree and listened to Lyle's voice, each word causing her to fall for the man just a little more.

Chapter 7

In the cab of the pickup truck, Cindy and Jimmy slept, Jimmy snoring like he always did.

In the rear bed, under the night sky, slept Sue, Raven and Henry.

But where the others' dreams were filled with lightheartedness; Henry's visions were filled with dark monsters and horrors best left in the dark.

His dream had him walking down a deserted highway, the pavement cracked and missing in places, as if a massive earthquake had picked up the blacktop and had then dropped it back to the earth.

The asphalt was riddled with cracks and in these cracks grew all manner of plants. Kudzu, goldenrod and brown-eyed Susans all burst through the cracks in a massive profusion of vegetation.

Henry climbed over the worst of the ravaged road, always wary of turning an ankle. As he walked, he reached down for his weapons and was surprised to see they were missing. Both holster and sheath were there but the weapons that should be within were gone. As he looked around, he didn't understand why he was alone. Where were his traveling companions? Where was Jimmy?

No knowing what to do, he continued onward, pushing past the worst of the foliage as he made his way down the devastated road.

He walked for what seemed like miles, the austere landscape on both sides of the highway nothing but desert. And then he came upon the rusted out gates of what appeared to be an old cemetery.

With no end in sight to the ruined highway, he turned off and entered the cemetery, hoping there might be something inside he could use to help him, or maybe a well with fresh water.

Large tombstones, stone angels and graceful ministers with dew on their faces, making them look as if they were weeping mournful tears for the dead, filled the rows from left to right.

They surrounded him on all sides, each one with names and dates, the virtues of a husband, father, brother who lay buried there etched for all eternity.

His feet sank a half inch in the cropped turf, feeling like he was walking on a massive sponge. Squishing sounds could be heard as he walked, moisture rising up around each footfall to leave the impression of his path until the turf pushed back to wipe the slate clean.

One marker caught his attention, so he paused to look at it. Kneeling down to read the inscription, he was shocked to see his name carved into the faded marble.

Henry Watson, he died in agony and now walks with the dead.

As he stood up, not wanting to read anymore, he saw the next grave was etched with the same words, and the one after that and it seemed each one for as far as he could see.

Turning, he began to run and soon it seemed the markers had changed, other anonymous names taking the place of his. He slowed down and walked slower, careful where he placed his feet, not wanting to end up in an open grave, buried before his time.

As he moved through the cemetery, the first gnarled tree on his right stared down at him. On its branches were hundreds of crows, each glaring at him with dark, beady eyes. They shifted back and forth and side to side on the bent limbs as they ruffled their wings, a few cawing at him.

Below them, on the ground, the earth was covered in bird shit, attesting to how long the crows had been sitting there.

Not wanting to stir them, Henry moved past the tree and continued deeper into the graveyard.

The gravestones were covered in moss and fungus, looking like they were hundreds of years old. Discarded flowers and other signs of visitors were now rotted and decayed, perhaps resembling the bodies interred in the ground.

When he reached the middle of the cemetery, he saw the gravestones were laid out in a circular pattern, spreading out from the middle.

In the middle of this pattern, was an ancient oak tree, covered with black shapes that looked to be more than a hundred years old. The bark was more than three feet wide, the diameter double that, and its tree branches were so heavy in some places they dropped to the earth, touching the grass and actually becoming covered with soil.

But that wasn't what was so disturbing about this tree.

In the darkness, Henry wasn't sure at first what he was seeing, but as the clouds shifted overhead, allowing the moonlight to wax down, he saw the dark shapes come into focus.

And he realized they were human bodies.

More than two dozen corpses were hanging from the tree, large spikes through their hands and feet, their heads lolling to the sides, their frail necks too weak to hold them up. Maggots crawled and wiggled inside open wounds that seeped yellow and brown pus. The ichor covered the trampled lawn like dew, making a ring around the tree where odd-colored mushrooms grew, feeding off the bile and pus.

Perched on the shoulders of many of these lost souls were more crows, their beaks covered in a dark ichor that had to be dried blood. As the corpses hung like ornaments on a death tree, the crows would dart in and pluck a juicy eye from a socket, gobbling the orb whole.

One crow sat on the shoulder of a corpse, worrying at the dried lips. As it pulled with its beak, the lips parted and stretched, reminding Henry of Gummy Worms or an old rubber band. With a slap, the lips snapped free and the crow flew to another limb to devour its prize, a few caws let loose in victory.

Henry stood motionless, staring at the unbelievable sight, when one of the bodies to the right began to twitch like electricity was flooding its system. The arms and legs began to flail madly as the head jumped back and forth.

And then, the strength of the spasms became so great that the right hand was ripped from its spike, spraying dark blood out and across the lawn. Soon, the other hand was free, and with nothing to support its upper body, the corpse fell straight down like an ironing board. As the body dropped, the spikes holding the feet could not support it and the flesh was ripped in half, the feet now free of the tree.

With both its feet now in two pieces, similar to massive hooves, the corpse lay on the ground, writhing in what to Henry seemed to be unbelievable pain.

Slowly, the head rose and the dead eyes bore into Henry like lightning bolts. He was rooted to the spot, as if somehow the living corpse had hypnotized him to remain in place.

As Henry stared immobile, the corpse pushed itself onto its elbows and opened its mouth wide.

A piercing scream left those parched lips, like a siren call to the undead.

Like a light switch was flicked, every corpse on the hangman's tree began to jump and spasm, hands tearing from the spikes in bloody rivers of dark blood.

One at a time they dropped to the earth, to wallow on the ground like large slugs. More than one had snapped an arm or leg in its fall and now bone protruded; the white glistening in the moonlight.

Slowly but methodically, each corpse came to its feet, swaying back and forth as if each heard a symphony. And perhaps they did.

A symphony of the dead.

As the first ghoul opened its mouth yet again and let out a shrieking scream that curdled the blood, each of the others joined in, motioning and wailing at the unjust way they had died.

Henry, still locked in paralysis, realized if he didn't run now, he would quickly find himself swallowed alive by this horde of lost souls.

With every ounce of willpower, he forced the spell over him to break. He tried to move his right leg but it was like it was strapped down to a table, iron bands holding it firm. Still, he refused to give up and with sweat pouring down his brow, he strained to move his leg, all the while the crowd of undead corpses was slowly making its way to his position.

With a groan of pain, he got his leg to move. It was only an inch, but an inch nonetheless. With another surge of strength, he managed to move another inch, and soon that became two, and three and so on.

Then he was walking, foot by plodding foot, the paralysis slowing him but not stopping him.

And he found the more he distanced himself from that first ghoul, the less his limbs resisted when he made them move.

Before he knew it, he was running, dashing through the cemetery as the horde of ghouls followed behind.

He passed by the angels and markers to enter yet another part of the cemetery.

Here the trees were older still. Some stunted yew trees, their knobbed branches draped with fronds of Spanish moss, weaved together to form an impenetrable barrier. More oak and pine trees lined the graveyard, their bark torn and shredded as if claws had attacked and attempted to slice into the trunk with nothing but brute power.

There was a low mist now, too, and as Henry moved from marker to gravestone, he saw the pale moonlight falling on him didn't allow him to cast a shadow, though everything else did.

It was like he wasn't really there, that he was just a ghost.

Behind him, he heard the moans of the dead and he turned and walked faster, not wanting to be overtaken by them. Here, many of the tombstones had fallen, some breaking, the jagged tips now lying in the soft loom, waiting to trip the unwary.

Still he moved, slowly picking his way along the graves as the undead moaned and wailed behind him. A chill went down his spine as he thought what would happen if he let them catch him, and it drove him onward at a faster rate.

So he ran on, weaving through the angels that peered down at him as if with contempt. The fog grew thicker and he had to fight for every step, his vision down to barely a few feet. And all along, the dead followed, their wails caressing his back, causing the hairs on the back of his neck to stand on end.

The ground rose and fell like a massive ribbon, each step becoming harder to take. Henry had to pause a few times as he peered into the rolling fog bank that seemed to have enveloped everything.

Then, over the sounds of the undead, he heard another sound, one of water lapping the shore. At first he didn't know which way to go, so he cocked his head, straining with his ears, his mouth open. And then he had the way and he took off at a ground-eating sprint, jumping over graves and hurtling stone markers.

Before he reached what he believed was salvation, his foot came down on empty air and he found himself tumbling into an open grave.

He fell for a fraction of a second, and then he was underwater. The grave had filled with muddy, putrid water and he flailed about as he tried to stay on the surface.

He swam to the edge, as it should only be a few feet in any direction, but as he wadded through the water, the edge didn't appear, nor did his hands feel the muddy soil.

From below he felt things grab at his feet and he let out a soft yell as he kicked harder, sliding free of whatever terror lurked within its murky depths.

Laughter came to his ears and he spun in the water, searching for the origination, but there was nothing, only the swirling fog to hide anything and everything. More laughter and he looked up, wondering if it was coming from above.

The fog was playing tricks and it was difficult to gauge the direction. Deciding he would tire if he merely treaded water, he headed off in a direction, praying it was the correct one. At least he'd left the walking dead behind, he figured.

He swam for what felt like hours, or was simply minutes, time having no meaning, but eventually he reached the shore. Waterlogged and exhausted, he crawled out on the muddy shore, his arms feeling like lead weights.

And then the laughter came again, high-pitched and shrill. Perking up, he looked for a weapon but there was nothing on the beach but a few tawdry branches that would snap the second he hit an opponent with it.

And then he saw the shadows as they coalesced out of the fog and stepped onto the beach. He knew they were the same ones, though now their faces were gone, only pale skulls replacing the charnel house visages. Hands were curled into claws, and the dead flexed them in preparation for peeling the flesh from Henry's body.

And then one stepped out from the others, and Henry assumed this was the leader. This one was death incarnate, with a face of rotting flesh, the skin sliding off in large chunks from the scabrous bone beneath.

Behind him, Henry heard the water churn, and when he glanced behind him, he peered into the fog to see something large break the surface of the water. It was dark black and from the brief glimpse he had, it reminded him of an electric eel, only fifty times the size. He knew he wouldn't be going back into the water to escape the walking dead.

The leader of the dead took a step forward and as the fog lifted, the face was seen clearly for a second. When the figure stepped out and walked closer to Henry, he saw it was the face of his wife, Emily.

Her complexion was perfect, her eyes wide and kind, her lips curled up into a slight grin. But he saw loss there too, and he remembered what he'd had to do to her that fateful day two years ago.

"Henry, wake up, you need to wake up," she whispered softly, almost as if it was nothing more than a gentle breeze.

He opened his mouth to say something, to tell her how much he loved her, how much he missed her, but before he could, she raised one skeletal finger to her lips and shook her head.

"Not now, my love, another time, when the moment is right, but remember that I'm always with you. Now, wake up, your friends need you."

She stepped back, the other undead moving with her, and as one they flowed into the fog and were gone. Henry stood, watching the shapes dissolve, his heart breaking over his lost love all over again.

In the rear of the pickup, his eyes snapped open and he was gazing up at the star-filled night sky.

He didn't know what had woken him, but as he let out a breath and tried to retain some of the dream, he heard a soft noise, as of a very tiny twig breaking.

Coming to a sitting position, he was surprised to feel refreshed, as if he'd slept for half a day instead of only a few hours.

As his eyes scanned the darkness, he filtered out Jimmy's snoring and then heard it again.

Snap.

Climbing out of the pickup, and careful not wake, Sue, Raven, Jimmy and Cindy, as he didn't know if there was cause for alarm yet, he walked through the small glade they were parked in. He pushed aside some of the branches they set up as an alarm, and then went out to the road.

Snap, he heard it again.

Crossing the road, in the gloom of night, he found himself standing over the zombie he'd killed earlier. And when he waited for the next snap, he spotted the severed head.

Leaning down, he picked up the head and was more than a little surprised to see the severed head was chewing on the small carcass of a mouse. The teeth were grinding the head to pulp and the molars attempted to position the mouse to be swallowed. Which of course was ridiculous as there was nowhere for the chewed mouse to go after it was swallowed. The snaps he heard were each time a small mouse bone was cracked by yellow teeth.

Disgusted, he tossed the head deeper into the woods, just glad to have it out of his line of sight, and as he turned to go back to the camp, he found himself staring at the grim, pale faces of two walking corpses.

One was a big one, over six feet, with wide shoulders and muscular arms. If Henry had to guess, he would have assumed the dead man had been into steroids before being killed and returning as a ghoul.

The other was a woman, five-five with perky breasts thanks to the bra she wore under a red shirt that had the word ***FOXY*** in gold stitching. She had a figure that would make any man slam on the brakes of his car. And even with half her face missing and her lower torso hanging off in flaps of skin, she was actually still attractive.

Not wanting to shoot for fear of calling any more undead onto his and the others position, Henry drew his panga from its sheath and prepared to fight hand to hand with the two ghouls.

He didn't have to wait long.

Hungry for fresh meat, Steroids dove in, teeth gnashing empty air in preparation of sinking them into Henry's neck. But Henry wasn't about to sit still and let the ghoul have at it and the panga slashed to the side, taking off the right hand and partially severing the left. Black ooze that was once blood seeped out of the jagged stump and the zombie moaned in annoyance.

As Henry fought with Steroids, Foxy came at him with a snarl. Her blonde hair was matted and it looked like a bird had nested there. She wasn't as big as Steroids but she was still dangerous. Henry took a step back to give himself some clearance and when she lunged for him, his panga was there, singing its song of death as it carved the air.

The sixteen inches of cold steel slid into her torso, and when Henry twisted and pulled up, the blade performed a vivisection that had her dried internal organs, intestines especially, spilling out before her. But this did nothing to slow her and Henry, acting fast, pulled up with the handle, the blade going through her sternum and ribcage to finish just below her Adam's apple if she was a man.

With one more heave, he ripped upward, the blade slicing her head in half, the rotting, soft skull no match for the razor-sharp steel of the panga. As blood and ichor splashed into the night air, Foxy dropped dead for good.

As soon as Henry freed his blade, Steroids was coming in for more. Henry spun and used his right boot to kick out and send Steroids falling backwards. But the zombie was big and it only slowed it for a second.

But that was all Henry needed. As he pivoted on his left foot, there was a large fallen tree on his right and Henry spun and jumped onto it, the added height now giving him a foot on Steroids.

As the large, lumbering ghoul charged him, Henry raised the panga over his head, and when the ghoul reached him, he brought the blade straight down, sliding through the skull and into the torso, the hilt touching the top of the skull. Steroids wobbled on his feet, looking like he had a large pin in the top of his head, but the blade had sliced through enough brain to shut down the electrics and the ghoul tumbled forward like a small tree.

A tiny puff of dust rose from the clothing as the ghoul hit the forest floor, and Henry jumped off the log to retrieve his panga.

It was so deep into the head and torso that it took him sitting on the ground with a boot on each shoulder, and both hands on the hilt of the panga, to free it. Then he yanked and pulled and slowly worked the blade free, for all purposes looking like King Arthur trying to free the fabled sword.

When he finally finished and had pulled his panga free of the corpse, he was exhausted and he quickly wiped the panga clean on the back of Steroids' pants and shirt.

With one last glance at the two very dead ghouls, he turned and went back to the campsite.

Checking his wristwatch, he saw he had another hour before he was supposed to relieve Mary, but he was so wired from the fight he decided he might as well just relieve her now. Then she could get some rest as he knew he was done sleeping for the night.

As he walked back across the road to the campsite, he heard a night bird call out from the tree tops. Maybe it was his imagination, but it sounded a little like laughter.

With a slight chill to his bones, his dream now forgotten as dreams were wont to do, he headed back, pleased that something had stirred him from his slumber.

For if the two ghouls had managed to sneak up on them while they were sleeping and get past the branches they had laid about the perimeter of the camp, who knew what might have happened.

Chapter 8

Mary and Lyle looked up as Henry came into view. They knew it was him or one of the others by the amount of noise he made as he worked his way to them. His boots crushed the leaves and twigs littering the forest floor without care, signaling he was walking through the trees.

When he appeared, Mary smiled as she always did upon seeing Henry. She idly noticed how different he looked from when she had met him almost two years ago. Back then, he had brown hair and a beer belly, though his upper body was still powerful thanks to an active younger life. But now, though in his forties, he resembled a man half his age. With his ash gray hair, he held an air of dignity, but his rock hard abs and muscular upper torso belayed that image. Henry had morphed into a warrior of the new world; hard like stone, a killer in his own right if need be. But Mary also knew there was till a merciful side of Henry that hadn't been beaten from him. He was the most honorable man she knew and she loved him like a father.

Lyle shifted next to her and she glanced to him. "That's weird, Henry's early," she said.

Lyle shrugged, not knowing anything about the nuances and dynamics of the group. Henry moved close enough to speak without his voice carrying too far, and he flashed her a polite smile in greeting.

"Hey, honey, want to get relieved early?"

"Really?" Mary asked. "I have another hour left on my watch."

Henry shrugged. "Yeah, I know, but I woke up early so I might as well let you get some rest. I don't plan on sleeping anymore."

Mary didn't hesitate with an answer. "That would be great, Henry, thanks," she grinned. She leaned over and kissed him on the cheek.

"It's been quiet so far. I thought I heard something a minute or so ago over by the road but it was gone before I could pinpoint it. Figured it was an animal or something," she told him.

Henry thought back to the ghoul he'd taken down and shrugged again. "It must have been an animal, it's all quiet over there. I should know, I was just there. Besides, we have all these branches around the perimeter. Anything tries to get through, we'll hear it coming from a mile away."

"Oh, okay, sounds good then," she replied.

Henry turned to Lyle who hadn't said a word.

"So why are you with her?" He asked like a protective father but Lyle was unfazed.

"I was restless so I thought I'd give her some company. Not a problem, is it?"

Henry shook his head no. "Hey, she's a big girl; she can do what she wants with whoever she wants."

Mary frowned. "Uh, excuse me, gentleman, but I'm standing right here. I'd appreciate it if you wouldn't pretend I'm not."

Henry chuckled. "Sorry, honey, didn't mean anything by that." He shifted position slightly, his hand going to his panga out of habit. "Look, I got this, why don't you go and get that rest. You, too, Lyle. If we're going to your town in the morning, then we've got a long day ahead of us. Who knows what's gonna be on the way there."

Lyle nodded, as did Mary.

"Okay, Henry, thanks, see you in the morning," Mary waved and moved away from him. Lyle merely nodded to Henry curtly, the older man replying in the same fashion.

The entire encounter had been done in the darkness, only the stars to illuminate their faces. Many of the nuances had been lost amongst each of them as visibility was low. Still, Henry sensed the way Lyle was looking at Mary, the way his head would lean toward her while they all talked, and he could only hope as the two walked away, that Mary knew what she was doing.

Chapter 9

Lyle caught up with Mary as she walked and touched her arm to slow her.

"Mary, wait, I was wondering if you might go for a walk with me before you turn in."

Mary stopped walking and turned to look at him. His face was a dull shape in the night, but she could see the outline of his jaw and cheeks. Though she couldn't see his face, her mind filled in the blanks. And she liked what she saw.

"A walk, huh?" She gave it a moment's thought and nodded yes. Then realizing he couldn't see the gesture, she reached out and touched his arm. "Okay, sure, let's walk. I'm not ready to sleep yet anyway."

"Okay, great," he said, sounding like a teenager asking out a girl on a date. He pointed to a small path to the left of them that ran parallel with the stream. "Why don't we go that way? It looks like there's a small deer path."

"Okay, I'll lead," she said and he followed her, the two heading out. As they walked, they talked in low voices, sharing small tidbits of their lives before the world was overrun by the walking dead. They found out they were quite compatible and saw the world through similar eyes.

The path moved around boulders and large trees, meandering along the stream, until it came out overlooking a small beach, the stream rushing by.

Lyle stepped up next to her and he pointed at the stream. "That water looks inviting, how 'bout a dip?"

"No thanks, it's dark and I most certainty don't have a bathing suit."

Lyle knew this was true as each of the companions had bathed in their underwear or in nothing at all.

"That's okay, I don't mind," he replied. The moon came out when the cloud cover had broken, allowing more illumination. Now Mary could see Lyle's face better and what she saw was a smiling man.

"I was kind of thinking we could, you know, skinny dip."

She laughed then, and Lyle felt his insides flip at the sound, like a hundred butterflies were in his stomach. Her melodic voice was music to his ears.

"Skinny dip? Are you crazy? We're not sixteen, Lyle, and this isn't high school."

He stepped in close to her so they were less than six inches apart.

"I know that, Mary, but listen, this world we live in now, that man and his family we left back at the cannie camp. That right there should tell you what I'm thinking. This world, one second you're here the next you're not. We have to take pleasure where we can, 'cause the next second there might be nothing but death. I see the way you get along with Henry and the others. You guys have been out there, traveling about. You know what I'm saying is true."

"Lyle, I…I don't know what to say to that. Henry, Jimmy and the rest are my family now. I can't just abandon them."

He raised his right hand and clenched it into a fist, as he shook his head, his eyes closing slowly as if he was trying to explain something to a daft child.

"No, Mary, you're not listening to me. This isn't a long term thing I'm talking about, I just…"

But he never finished his sentence. Mary stepped up to him and kissed him passionately, wrapping her arms around his neck. At first he was unresponsive, not expecting her to take the initiative, but after recovering, he kissed her back, wrapping his arms around her as his left hand cupped the back of her neck. The two explored each others mouths, their passion growing as their hands rubbed and petted.

After two full minutes, Mary took a step back from him, but only a few inches. Their mouths were so close they could feel the exhale of the other and Mary sucked in a deep breath, trying to catch some air.

"I...I don't know what came over me. It's just...it's been almost two years, Lyle. I haven't been with anyone in over two years. I just broke up with my boyfriend and then the world fell apart. Since then, with Henry and the others, there's been no time for a relationship. We're always moving, running. Sometimes it's like we never stop. I..."

He reached up and touched her lips with his index finger.

"Mary, shhhh, you don't have to say anything. I don't need an explanation. None of it matters. All that matters is you and me, right now. Future, past, who gives a damn."

A tear slid down her cheek as she nodded, biting her lip slightly. Lyle reached out with his right thumb and cupped her face, brushing the tear away.

"What's that for? Why are you crying?"

"I...I'm sorry, I don't mean to act like such a *girl*, it's just...I haven't let my guard down in such a long time."

"Well, you can with me, Mary. I haven't met a woman like you in a long time, and that goes from before everything went to shit."

She stepped up to him again, his hand still on her cheek, and she tilted her head slightly, inviting him to kiss her. He took the offer and their lips touched again, tongues darting and exploring the warmth of the other.

As they began to kiss again, hands slowly began to explore one another as they started to undress. Shirts were first, followed by pants. It was rather amusing how Mary had to take off her gun, knife and a smaller knife she had in a pocket. Compared to Lyle, she was a walking arsenal and the two had a small chuckle about it. But then they were at each other again like two starving dogs feeding on a chunk of raw meat. It had been a long time for Lyle, also, and Mary was one of the most beautiful women he had ever met.

And as the two spread out their clothing like a blanket, he slowly laid her down, naked as the day she was born. She went with it, letting him lead, and as she stretched out on the ground, her back arcing so that the curves of her thighs flowed into her thin waist, her firm breasts tempting him, her nipples pointed with arousal, the small tuft of hair at the juncture of her thighs, her brown hair spread out around her head like that of an angel, he thought she resembled a porcelain sculpture.

Lyle gazed down at her. "My God, you're beautiful," he said as his eyes tried to soak in every inch of her firm, tight body.

"Shut up and come here," she said as her arms opened invitingly, letting herself go and doing like he said. She was living in the moment, and right now she wanted him.

He lay down next to her, maneuvering so that he was spooning with her. His hand reached over and cupped one of her breasts, his thumb and forefinger caressing the already hard nipple. He nibbled the back of her neck as he pressed his erection into the small of her back.

Mary, not shy about sex, reached around and began to caress his hard member, squeezing her fingers as she slowly stroked the shaft, making him moan softly in pleasure. Mary soon joined him as his teeth gently bit her neck, causing her to giggle and squirm with desire.

Lyle then shifted position and climbed on top of her, but before she could ask what was next, he began to slide down her body until his face was even with the dark coils of hair between her thighs. Mary giggled again but she opened herself to him, signaling that what he wanted to do was fine with her. Her left foot found his penis and she used the other to begin stroking it with the sole of her foot as Lyle gently parted her with his fingers and slid one finger inside her. Mary moaned, grabbing his hair and thrusting upward, burying his face into her as she gasped with passion.

She felt a fluttering in her stomach and then felt herself shudder. Her eyelids creased as Lyle's tongue flicked out, tasting her as he lapped at the softness that made her a woman. Her legs squeezed his head deeper into her as she let out a soft yelp of pleasure.

Though almost suffocating him as her legs pressed his face into her warmth, his ministrations continued for another two minutes until Mary couldn't take it any longer and she yanked on his hair, causing him to grunt in pain. But it was playful pain, and as he slowly crawled back to her, his face now wet with her desire, she kissed him hard as if her life depended on it.

Positioning himself between her, he slowly slid himself into her, the feeling so exquisite he saw flashes of light in his vision. His entire body was now nothing but his manhood as he slowly and surely began to pump in and out, Mary thrusting upwards each time to meet him.

The two became one for more than five minutes and Lyle was preparing to explode. He had no idea how far down the road Mary was, but he knew he couldn't last much longer. So, not wanting it to end so fast, he stopped and rolled off her.

"Just give me a second, okay? I want this too last for longer than five minutes. I don't want it to be too quick."

She sat up and came to her knees, a seductive smile on her face. "Oh, don't worry, it won't be," she said and slowly climbed on top of him, her head sliding down to his crotch. He held his breath, not believing what was happening to him as she opened her mouth and lowered her head down. He gasped as she swallowed him, sucking gently, her head now rising and falling in an even tempo. Lyle moaned in ecstasy, telling himself if he was to die right now, that he would die a very happy man.

When he felt like his dick was going to explode like a Cherry bomb, his entire body on the edge of a massive orgasm, she stopped and pulled her head up.

She looked into his eyes and shook her head sadly. "Oh, no Lyle, not yet, we'll go together or not at all."

She grinned like a banshee as she knelt over him, raised herself over his rock hard member and slowly lowered herself down on him.

Lyle pushed up like he was a jackhammer as she came down just as hard. Both their eyes were closed as each took pleasure from the other, the sounds of flesh slapping filling the air. He pulled her to him, their mouths locking as they passionately kissed, the two areas of contact electrifying, body parts gyrating, tongues exploring, flesh, now sweaty with excitement, rubbing tightly, as both of them felt themselves coming to the abyss.

Lyle hugged her tight, so tight that in the back of his mind he hoped he wasn't hurting her, but she barely noticed if he was, as she was lost in the rise of her second orgasm.

And then Lyle could hold back no longer, and with a grunt and a low moan, he arched his back and felt like his entire body was now exiting him through the small eye at the tip of his penis. He cried out in happiness but it was muffled, his face buried in her breasts as she dug her fingernails into the edges of his shoulders, leaving bruises that would remind him of this night for more than two weeks after it had passed.

And then she was shuddering against him as she threw her head back, her spine bending, her mouth opening and closing, and her eyes rolling back in her head.

She gasped one final time and bent forward, collapsing on him as she breathed in and out like she had run a mile in three minutes.

He hugged her tightly, and after a full minute, he shifted position so he could kiss her again. Reciprocating, she pressed her mouth to his, the two becoming one yet again.

When they had both calmed enough to think straight, Mary rolled off him but stayed next to him, unashamed at her exploits.

She laughed lightly as she saw the look on his face, the redness of his cheeks when she had pressed his face into her chest. She could have suffocated him, she thought.

"I'm so sorry; I guess I got carried away. I think I could have broken your neck and not even realized I'd done it. I think I was enjoying myself a little too much."

He shook his head, waving her words away. "If that's how I was gonna die, I can't think of a better way. Don't worry about it."

She curled up next to him, her right ear resting on his chest as she listened to his heartbeat slowly smoothing out, his breathing calming as his pulse returned to normal.

They stayed that way for all of fifteen minutes until the need for one another had returned. This time their lovemaking was gentler, their moves one of infinite slowness as each tried to please the other, now that their lust had been satiated.

As the moon slowly dropped from the sky and the dawn touched the horizon, they made love a total of three times, the last taking place in the stream as they washed up from their torrent of sex. After what happened to Jimmy, they made sure to stay close to the shore, where the water was shallow.

The water proved to make things more difficult, washing lubrication away and they finished on the shore as the sun slowly began to rise.

By the time the sun was in full bloom, the two were dressed again and sitting at the edge of the water talking, each feeling as spent as if they had traveled the entire breadth of the deadlands on foot and in one night. But despite this, both were full of energy at the same time, feeling as if they could take on an entire zombie horde with nothing but their fists.

What the two had experienced this night was worth a few hours of lost sleep, and when Mary leaned into him, Lyle's left hand gently brushed her hair.

She turned and looked up into his face. "This never happened, Lyle, you hear me? Henry and the others can never know."

He looked at her, perplexed, not understanding. "Why not?"

"Because it can't. Look, I have my reasons, okay? Jimmy would never let me hear the end of it and Henry…well, I just don't want him to know."

"I don't get it. If they're your friends, wouldn't they want you to be happy? You're human; don't you get to enjoy some of life, too? I see Cindy and Jimmy together; they're a couple, so why can't we be one, too?"

She pushed away from him and looked deep into his eyes.

"A couple? Tell me, Lyle, were you planning on coming with me when me and my friends leave your town?"

"No, of course not. Actually I was kind of hoping…"

She cut him off. "Exactly, but I know what you're gonna say and the answer is no. When Henry wants to go I go too. This was great, but it's what they used to call a one night stand." She frowned. "You said it yourself a few hours ago. No future and past, just now. Well, now's over and it's time to get back to the present."

He sighed heavily but as he returned her piercing gaze, he saw the fire there, the strength of her will, and he finally nodded, knowing there would be no changing her mind.

"Fine, Mary, you win, this never happened."

She stood up then as did he.

Picking up her weapons, she began to put them back on her person. When she was through, Lyle was watching her with his arms crossed, a smile creasing his lips.

"What?" she asked as she returned his smile.

"Nothing, Mary, nothing. I was just thinking. For something that never happened, you screw like a jackrabbit."

She sauntered over to him and kissed him lightly on the lips.

"Hey, it's not always you men who know all the tricks, you know. Some of us women know a thing or two, too."

"And how," he gasped, remembering her naked body spasming on his, the two of them pressed tightly together.

She slapped his shoulder playfully and he winced. There was a bruise there now thanks to Mary's fingernails.

She bit her lip. "Sorry, hurt much?"

"Nah, I'll live. It's a memento of our night and it was worth it. I'll be fine." He gazed up at the rising sun. "We should get back if you don't want anyone to know we've been gone."

She nodded and they took hands and walked back along the path. Just before they exited the path, they separated hands, and with one parting look, Mary stepped out into the glade by the stream and made her way back to the pickup truck and the others.

Lyle waited a moment and then made his way the long way around, the two working out this little plan to throw off suspicion that they had spent the night together. She knew she was being foolish, that Henry and the others would only want her to be happy, and that even Jimmy would be glad for her. His teasing wouldn't be that bad, but for some reason she had decided the time spent with Lyle was between the two of them and no one else needed to know about it.

As Mary walked through a strand of trees, she saw Henry talking to Jimmy and Sue. Cindy was near the edge of the stream, washing her face and getting them some much needed water, Raven helping her. With the stream flowing steadily, the current had washed away any remains of the ghoul that had attacked Jimmy, and the water was as fresh as a mountain spring. Cindy was still favoring her bad ankle but she was walking on it so it looked like she was on the way to a fast recovery.

Henry spotted Mary and he smiled at her. "Hey, sleep well?" he asked her as she moved up to within a few feet of him.

"Like a baby, all quiet?"

"Sure was. Just me, the night birds, and a few crickets. I thought I heard a couple of wolves or something rutting a ways down the stream but they were too far to see. It stopped eventually so they must have finished and moved on. Did you hear any of it?"

She felt herself growing beet red and she forced herself to act calm. "No, never heard a thing. So," she said changing the subject, "are we going to Cement City today?"

Henry nodded. "Sure, gotta go somewhere. Hey, you seen Lyle around?"

She was about to reply that no, she most certainly had not seen him, when Lyle stepped out of the forest.

"Hey, Henry, you call me? I heard my name. Sorry, I was watering Mother Nature. Answering the morning call and all that."

Henry turned to the side to see Lyle. Mary waited for Lyle to do or say something stupid but he didn't. He barely glanced at her, and when he did, he gave her a polite smile. "Morning, Mary," he said smoothly.

"Oh, uhm, morning Lyle. Sleep well?" she asked.

He nodded. "Like a baby, you?"

"Fine, fine."

"Okay, good, everyone slept great, so Lyle, what do you say we all grab some breakfast and then you take us to your town," Henry suggested.

Lyle slapped his hands together. "Sounds good to me, Henry. I'm looking forward to showing my home off. And after what you guys have been through lately, I bet a soft bed and a home cooked meal sounds pretty damn good."

"Lyle, you don't know the half of it," he said as he slapped Lyle on the shoulder, the younger man wincing but not showing his discomfort, as the two men walked off, heading to the pickup truck. Jimmy moved over to them and the three began chatting.

Mary waited a minute as the men joined up. Something inside her wondered if she wanted Lyle to break their agreement. For some reason the way he had acted, doing exactly what she had asked him now seemed wrong and she was having second thoughts.

But she knew she was right. He wasn't going to leave with them and she knew she wasn't going to stay in Cement City with him, so though the night was wonderful, a clean break was the best for both of them.

Still, *what ifs* plagued her.

"Mary, you all right? You look like you have something on your mind," Sue said from beside her. Mary had been so caught up in watching Lyle, she hadn't realized Sue was there.

"Huh? Oh, I'm fine, Sue, it's all good with me. You?"

"I'm fine, I'm going to help get breakfast ready," she said and with a small wave, moved off.

"Okay, I'll come help in a minute," Mary called. "I'll see if Cindy needs anything first."

"Okay," Sue replied.

With one more look at Lyle and a soft sigh of what might have been, Mary went to help Cindy as she filled their canteens, then they would eat quickly and get back out on the road.

At least she knew soon they would all be inside strong walls and they could relax for a time. And who knew? Maybe she and Lyle could get together for one or two more nights of passion.

With that pleasant thought in her mind, she picked up her pace, feeling a lot better than a second ago.

Chapter 10

An hour later, the group was back on the road again, the worn tires of the pickup truck eating up the miles on the weed-infested road. Kudzu and crabgrass were the worst of it, though a fine layer of moss had begun to grow out from the edges.

In many places the forest had grown onto the road, shrinking the two lane road down to just one. Another year or two and the road would become impassable, unless someone wanted to go out there and cut back the foliage.

Henry, Mary, Sue and Lyle were in the rear bed of the truck, while Jimmy drove and Cindy sat next to him in the cab, with Raven in the shotgun seat.

For Mary the ride was uncomfortable. She kept expecting Henry to blurt out that he knew everything, that he had heard Lyle and her making love the previous night and that he was ashamed of her. She didn't know why she felt this way. After all, didn't she deserve to find someone, too? To be happy, even if was just for a little while?

She glanced at Lyle, who only nodded to her curtly. He was as good as his word, not showing her any more attention than before they had spent the night together.

It looked like her secret was safe. The only question was whether she wanted it to stay that way.

Behind the wheel, Jimmy tapped Cindy on the shoulder.

"Hey, babe, you got any water in that canteen?"

She nodded and handed it to him. He took it and popped the top. He was preparing to drink some as she said, "Sure do, I topped them all off in the stream before we left."

Jimmy stopped the canteen just before it touched his lips.

"Wait a sec. Are you saying you filled this canteen in the stream?"

"Yeah, so what if I did? I didn't see a 7-ll nearby so it had to do, why?"

"Why? Cindy, don't you understand what kind of water this is?"

She looked at him with an obtuse glare, not getting where he was going with his line of talk.

"Jimmy, it's just water, shut up and drink it," she snapped, not in the mood for his jokes.

"But Cindy, there's fish in that stream, right?"

"Yes, I believe you're right in that assumption. So?"

"So? Cindy, baby, fish are fucking in that stream. I don't want to drink water that fish fuck in, that's nasty."

She frowned slightly, but then it slowly curled up into a grin.

"You're not really serious, are you?"

He tried to keep a straight face but in less than five seconds his visage cracked and he smiled. "Nah, I was just messin' with ya. Hell, if fish are getting it on then maybe if I drink this some of it might rub off on me and you." He drove around a pile of wrecked vehicles, anything worth salvaging long gone.

"And what does that mean exactly?" Cindy asked.

"Nothin' babe, it's just things have been a little dry in the sex department lately, that's all."

"Hello, teenager over here," Raven said as she rolled her eyes, becoming grossed out. Jimmy ignored her.

Cindy scooted up closer to him. She glanced at Raven to see the black-haired girl was staring out the window, doing her best to ignore the couple sitting beside her. Seeing the coast was clear, Cindy slid her hand into Jimmy's waistband, then inside his pants. Jimmy began to choke on the water and he stuck the cap back on, not able to handle so many distractions while he drove.

"Well, baby, we can fix that right here," she breathed into his ear.

"Are you serious?" His voice cracked a little.

Cindy was the kind of woman he would have only been able to get with in his dreams, but with the world what it was, old misconceptions were gone. The two now had a bond that went deeper than love. For over a year and a half they had been inseparable and Jimmy had been having the best sex of his life. Especially as this sex was with another person, not like back when he'd been working at Pineridge Labs and was a loner.

Cindy pulled her hand out and tapped Raven on the shoulder with her other one. "Can you go in back and give us a few minutes to talk alone?"

Raven glanced at her, then at Jimmy. She saw his flushed cheeks and how his eyes were wide with excitement. Making a disgusted face she said, "Gonna talk huh? Fine, it would be my pleasure." Without waiting for Jimmy to slow down, she crawled out the window and over the cab, dropping lightly into the rear bed. Henry asked her what was wrong and she said she wanted to get some air. He let it go without asking further as he was in a conversation with Lyle and Sue, Mary sitting quietly and listening.

Jimmy glanced in the rearview mirror to see Henry's left side pressed against the back window, and he realized no one could see into the cab of the pickup truck from the rear bed.

"Okay, babe, have at it," he grinned as she slowly leaned over into his lap.

Jimmy leaned back in the seat and did his best to concentrate on the road.

Thanks to his girlfriend, the boring ride to Cement City just became a lot more interesting.

Chapter 11

The tires and grille of the pickup truck was covered in a warm coating of blood and gore. Stuck inside the top corner of the grille, a scalp sizzled on the radiator, a piece from one of more than two dozen ghouls Jimmy had run down on their trek thus far.

In groups of twos and threes, the ghouls had wandered the road, and with manic glee, Jimmy had made sure to leave them less mobile after he passed them by.

Jimmy slowed as he rounded a bend in the road and Henry leaned over and asked what was wrong. Then he looked forward and received his answer.

From shoulder to shoulder, the road was clogged with bodies, nearly fifty of them from a quick count, all strewn about, lying in odd angles.

Jimmy stopped fifty feet from the first bloated corpse, the engine ticking softly as the companions stared at the carnage before them.

"What the hell is this?" Henry whispered as he stood in the rear bed, his arms leaning on the roof of the cab, and let his eyes play over the bodies. Men, women and children of all ages were scattered about. Arms and legs were missing and the stench of rotting meat filled the air. Luckily, for the moment, the wind was blowing the opposite way.

"It looks like a massacre happened here," Sue said by his side. "Oh my God, so many bodies."

Henry turned to look at Lyle. "You know anything about this?"

Lyle shook his head no. "The only thing I can think of is they were travelers, refugees maybe, and they were trying to get to Cement City."

"Well, it doesn't look like they made it, does it?" Henry said in a low voice.

Jimmy opened his door and stood on the floorboard so he could get a better view of the corpses. "Hey, Henry, I don't see any shell casings. I don't think those people were shot."

Henry reached into his backpack and pulled out his binoculars. He scanned the bodies, studying each one. "You're right. I don't see anything that looks like bullet holes. There should be some sign if they'd been shot down."

"Then what did it?" Mary asked. "What could have killed all those people?"

Henry shook his head. In the end, it didn't matter how they died. It wasn't his problem. The only thing he needed to worry about was getting his people to Cement City safely.

"Doesn't matter," he told Mary. "Dead is dead." He leaned over to Jimmy who was still standing half-in and half-out of the pickup. "Think you can drive through them?"

Jimmy shrugged. "Shit, Henry, I don't see why not. It might get messy, though. Some of them look pretty ripe."

"That's irrelevant. All I want to know is if the pickup can get through there."

"Sure," Jimmy replied. "It'll be slippery, but the tires can handle it easily. Gonna be gross, though."

"I think we can all handle *gross*, don't you, Jimmy?" Henry asked wryly.

"I didn't say we couldn't, old man. Still, it's gonna be nasty."

"Just get goin'. The sooner we're through, the sooner we'll be on our way again."

"You got it. Hold on tight back there. I don't think anyone wants to pick this spot to fall off when I'm driving through there, if you know what I mean."

He slid back behind the wheel and looked at Cindy and Raven, the latter having joined them in the cab earlier. "You girls ready to get nasty?"

"Just drive," Raven said in an annoyed tone.

"She's got a point, Jimmy, let's get this over with," Cindy said. Her nose was wrinkled as she stared at the corpses. She was disgusted by the carnage. She could see crows feeding on the bodies, hopping from each one, tearing off ribbons of flesh, while other pulled gobbets of skin and meat to quickly swallow and go in for more. A thick cloud of black flies hovered over almost every corpse, crawling in and out of any opening available. And the stomachs, bloated and full of decomposing gas, undulated like a water balloon being carried in a box, the person carrying them walking heavily, causing them to shake. Like a heartbeat, the bellies pulsed with gas, in and out, in and out. Finally, Cindy had to look away or risk losing her breakfast, the feeding frenzy too much to bear.

Jimmy began driving forward, for once seeming to not be as cocky as he usually was.

As the pickup reached the first body, only the hand of the corpse was close to the front left tire. Slowly, Jimmy drove over the hand.

Like firecrackers were going off, the hand snapped and popped as the weight of the vehicle cracked bones. In the rear of the bed, everyone was covering their mouths and noses from the redolence of death, constantly waving the flies away.

Jimmy slowed the pickup once more as if taking stock of the situation, and he glanced at Cindy who used her chin to gesture that he should keep moving.

As if he had to psych himself up, he pressed the gas pedal and the truck continued.

When the rear tire ran over the hand, the sound was lighter, as most of the bones had already been pulverized. But no sooner did the rear tire finish running over the hand, then the front tires were rolling over the next corpse in line.

As the right front tire went over the small corpse of a child, the tire sank six inches into its body cavity. Flies flew off, annoyed their meal was being disturbed, and the gasses trapped within the small corpse escaped, surrounding the pickup in a miasma of decay and rot.

"I think I'm going to be sick," Sue said from beside Henry in the rear of the pickup.

"You won't be the only one," Henry replied as he fought to keep down his breakfast. Though hardened to the redolence of death, the sickly sweet rot was like a living thing, the way it seeped into your sinuses and stuck to the back of your throat. He knew it would be more than a day before he could finally put the odor behind him.

Jimmy continued rolling through the piles of corpses, and he tried to focus on the road ahead.

Thirty feet away was the end of the carnage and the road was open once more. He and everyone else was so focused on the road ahead, that no one saw the first corpse move, the desiccated head swiveling to follow the pickup truck, the fingers on the first hand slowly twitching.

As the pickup carefully made its way throough the bodies, the tires popping corpses like balloons, the first of the fetid bodies began to rise up.

It was Raven who figured out something was wrong as she stared out into the horizon, not wanting to look at the bodies anymore than the others.

She caught movement out of the corner of her eye, and at first thought it was one of the dozens of crows or the thousands of flies. But when she let her gaze follow the movement, she was shocked to see one of the bodies sitting up. She blinked to make sure she wasn't imagining it, and when the body went to its knees, she knew they were in trouble.

"Jimmy," Raven said softly. "You need to get us out of here right now."

Jimmy, concentrating on driving through the obstacle of corpses, barely heard her and he glanced her way, wanting to ask her what she was saying. That was when his eyes focused straight out the front windshield and onto the road, not out into the distance.

One at a time, the bodies were coming to their knees, then standing, while behind the pickup, the zombies not damaged by the tires slowly rose as well.

"What the fuck?" Jimmy mumbled as he slowed the pickup to stare at the tableaux before and behind him.

The zombies were now on their feet, flowing together to block the road. Behind the vehicle, they were doing the same thing also. Some could only crawl, thanks to their torso becoming broken as the pickup drove over them, but they did their best to follow the undead crowd.

"Jimmy, get us out of here! It's a goddamn trap!" Henry yelled from the rear bed. Jimmy heard the distinctive double-tap of Henry's Glock and knew it was serious.

Coming out of his fugue state, he stepped on the gas to move again. The rear tires churned and spewed blood and gore and they spun inside the torso of a large, fat body. Like being stuck in mud, Jimmy could get no traction and the pickup's rear wheel drive spun and whirred.

"Jimmy, what are you doing? Go!" Henry yelled.

"I am! The damn thing's stuck!"

Cindy let out a small gasp of surprise as she stared out the front windshield. "How can this be? They were dead."

Jimmy snapped his head at her and said, "No shit, baby, but it looks like they changed their minds!"

The tires continued to spin and they swung back and forth as if they were on ice.

Pale hands reached the pickup and began to slap the hood, while in the rear bed, the four companions stuck out in the open began shooting anything that came too close.

Mary had her .38 so close to a zombie's face that when she fired, there was no traveling distance for the bullet from the gun to the target. There was an instant result. The head was so rotten and decayed it exploded from the force of the round, sending shards of skull and brains in all directions.

Lyle used his feet, kicking ghouls away as they tried to climb into the rear bed while beside him, Sue used her .22 to stop any ghoul that came too close. She stayed calm and only shot when they were so close she could smell each individual zombie.

She shot each one in the eye, the bullet then bouncing around and shredding the brain within. Sometimes the bullet escaped the skull to ricochet away.

Henry pulled his panga free with his left hand and began hacking and slashing, wanting to conserve ammunition if possible. As he shot a ghoul in the face, he turned and swung the machete, decapitating another zombie in one fluid motion. The head of the ghoul spun in the air, looking like a beach ball at a rock concert. It landed in the hands of another zombie, where the ghoul looked at it for a moment, wondering what it was. Then it dropped the severed head to the blood-soaked ground and continued trying to reach the companions.

"Jimmy! Anytime is good!" Henry yelled as he kicked a mother of three in the face. The female zombie's jaw shattered, allowing the tongue to hang down like a neck tie. Flopping back and forth, it resembled an eel, the tongue now black and slimy.

"What the fuck do you think I'm trying to do?" Jimmy yelled back. "The damn tires are slipping."

"Try another gear," Cindy suggested. "Go backwards then forwards like it was snow."

He looked at her, as if her idea was stupid, but then he did what she suggested. The truck bucked and jumped and the four warriors in the back had to pause in their defense to hold on.

Cindy jumped in her seat when a zombie slapped the passenger window. Raven only stared impassively, knowing the glass would hold. Pus and slime was left on the glass as the zombie banged to get at the three people within the vehicle.

Jimmy put the transmission into reverse and slowly began to back up. More gore sprayed into the air and the tires began to spin anew. But the different angle of rotation caused the bodies beneath the wheels to shift, and before Jimmy knew it, the tires were on the road once more. He slammed the transmission into drive again and began driving forward.

A dozen hands slapped the metal of the fenders as the pickup began moving through the crowd of bloated bodies. The sky was blocked out as the thousands of flies hovered overhead, waiting for their meals to stop moving.

"Everyone hold on!" Henry yelled to the others beside him. "Jimmy, punch it, get us the hell out of here!"

Jimmy heard Henry through the moans, banging, gunshots and wails and he placed a hand on Cindy's leg to warn her. "Hold on, baby, this is gonna get rough."

He floored the gas pedal, the pickup surging forward, punching through the line of zombies. Bodies flew off in all directions and if they were more closely packed, the momentum of the pickup wouldn't have been enough to let it break free. But it did get free and half a minute later, the last zombie was knocked to the road with a broken leg as the pickup left the ghouls behind.

Henry sat in the rear bed, staring out behind him. He saw the zombies turn and try to follow, but as the vehicle swung around a bend in the road, the ghouls were lost from sight.

Finally relaxing, he checked his Glock to see how many bullets he had and began wiping his panga clean with an old rag found in the bottom of the rear bed.

"What the hell just happened?" Mary asked as she sat down beside Lyle. For the moment, she didn't care about secrets, she just wanted to be next to someone.

Henry shook his head. "I have an idea but it's not something I want to accept," he said as he slid his now clean panga into its leather sheath.

"What, Henry, what do you think?" Sue asked and went to his side. He took her hand and squeezed it, kissing the back of it lovingly. He thanked God they had all made it out of there intact. Other than expending some ammunition, they were no worse for wear.

Henry sighed. He turned and slapped the roof of the pickup, signaling that Jimmy pull over. They were more than a mile from the zombies and the road was empty in both directions, only a few stray soda pop cans to mar the perfect landscape.

"Wait till we're all together. I don't want to have to repeat myself," Henry said as Jimmy pulled over and hopped out of the cab. Cindy stayed inside. Her ankle was healing and it wasn't worth putting weight on it. Raven climbed out, too, careful not to touch the sides of the truck, which were now covered in pus and gore.

"What's up, Henry?" Jimmy asked. "That was messed up back there, huh?"

"Yeah, Jimmy, that's why I had you stop. I have an idea what just happened and I don't think any of you are gonna like it."

"So spill it," Jimmy said as he scratched his nose.

"All right, fine. Here it is. I think those deaders back there were waiting for whatever came along. It was a trap. They were playing dead and once someone such as us drove into them, they closed the trap so they could kill and eat the poor bastards unlucky enough not to escape."

"That's crazy, Henry," Mary said. "It has to be some kind of co-incidence. Maybe they died and were just coming back when we got there."

"No, Mary, I thought of that, but the way everything happened was way too precise."

"So, what are you sayin'?" Jimmy began. "You think they were actually waiting for us? That they were smart enough to set a trap and then close it?"

"Yeah, I do, and I'll tell you what. If that's true, and the deaders are getting smarter, then we're all in trouble."

The only advantage we've had so far is that they're stupid. If they begin to think, he shrugged. "Well, that changes the entire game."

"So what do we do?" Sue asked.

Henry shook his head. "There's nothing we can do. All we can do is adapt and deal with it."

"And if we don't?" Cindy asked from inside the pickup.

Henry's face was grim as he leaned forward so he could look her in the eyes. "Then we're all dead."

Chapter 12

By the time the pickup truck pulled up at the makeshift wall surrounding the town of Cement City, all the companions were exhausted.

Other than the trap made by the walking dead, the rest of the ride to the town was uneventful. But just thinking about what Henry had suggested weighed heavily on all of them.

If the ghouls were becoming more intelligent, and were reasoning, then it didn't bode well for the remaining humans.

Jimmy slowed as he reached the gate, seeing that the men on the wall with an assortment of firearms were now aimed at them.

Lyle jumped down as soon as the pickup stopped and jogged over to the gate to speak to the men on watch.

As Lyle did this, Henry also climbed down from the rear bed of the pickup, his eyes taking in the ten foot high wall.

Though there was a mishmash of odds and ends mixed into the wall, the name of the town was easily established by the contents of the large barricade.

Cement was the main ingredient, as well as car parts, tires and steel rods. It wasn't pretty, but it served the town well. As Henry studied the wall in detail, he could see numerous pockmarks from stray rounds.

Off to the right was a large ditch where the stench of rotting bodies emanated. This was where the town disposed of the ghouls that arrived to try and get inside.

After being put down, the bodies were dragged to the ditch and discarded. Henry had seen this many times in his travels. When the ditch was full, it would be filled in and another, new ditch, would be dug to begin the process again.

As the months rolled by, dozens of these mass graves would dot the landscape outside the town. It was distasteful, but was now a part of life in the deadlands of new America.

Henry, Sue and Mary gathered next to Cindy and Jimmy. Cindy's ankle was doing well and she could stand on it easily as well as walk around. In another day or so she would be able to run on it. Raven stayed by the pickup, her arms crossed as she studied the wall.

"What do you think, old man?" Jimmy asked Henry as he studied the wall and the men on it.

Henry shook his head, not having an answer. "Looks like a dozen other towns we've visited over the past year," Henry replied.

"Think it's safe?" Mary asked, her hand touching the handle of her .38 out of instinct.

"We'll just have to wait and see. Let your boyfriend do the talking and get us inside," Henry said, his eyes never leaving the wall or the men standing on top of it.

Mary took on a look as if she'd been insulted. "Lyle's not my boyfriend, Henry. Whatever did you say that for?"

Henry shrugged. "It's just a joke, Mary. I saw the way he was looking at you last night. He likes you, is all."

Mary hid her relief that Henry didn't know anything about Lyle and her.

"Well, I'm not interested, Henry, you should know that right now. I'm perfectly happy with the way things are."

"Hey," Henry said, holding his hands up in surrender. "It's all fine with me. Whatever you want to do, Mary, you're a big girl."

"Hey, Henry," Jimmy called. "Lyle's waving us over to him."

Henry looked to where Lyle was standing at the wall and he turned and strode over to him; Mary, Jimmy and Cindy right behind him. Sue stayed with Raven. When they were next to Lyle, the man pointed up at the guard looking down on them while four other guards did the same from the sides.

"Henry, this is Ben, he's the head of security for the town."

"He looks like a cop," Jimmy said as he stared up at Ben.

Jimmy had a point. Ben wore his hair military style, cut close to the scalp. He was clean-shaven with no earrings in his ears and his face held a stern look, like a man who was used to being obeyed. If the man had been wearing a police uniform, he would have fit into it perfectly.

"That's 'cause I was one for ten years before all this shit happened. Why, that an issue for you?" Ben asked.

Jimmy shrugged. "Not at all, Officer, just as long as you don't want to bust my balls for not having a license on me, we're good," Jimmy replied sarcastically with a wide smile.

"That's enough, Jimmy, this is serious," Henry growled under his breath.

"I'll let you go with a warning this time," Ben said with a slight grin that said this was far from the truth. Henry assessed the man immediately and decided this was a man where the lines between black and white were solid. There would be no gray area in the middle. Henry had met men like Ben before and he didn't care for them—too rigid.

"Okay, so listen up, if you six want into my town then you need to relinquish your firearms."

Henry shook his head. "Ain't gonna happen, friend. Our weapons stay with us."

Ben frowned and looked to the guards on either side of him, nodding to each one.

Suddenly there was the rattle of weapons as each man on the wall aimed their guns at the companions. No sooner was this happening, then Henry and the others did the same, fingers on triggers but no one firing.

Jimmy moved up next to Henry and whispered out of the side of his mouth. "What the fuck, Henry? I thought these assholes were friendly?"

"Me too, Jimmy, but we're not giving up our guns. Every time we do it only spells trouble."

"So what do we do?" Mary asked, askance of him.

"We wait. Tell Cindy and Sue to hold their fire," Henry told her. Mary stepped behind him to inform the two women.

"What the fuck, Lyle?" Ben said to him. "I thought you said these people were cooperative."

"They are, Ben, now come on, lower your damn guns. I just told you a second ago these people saved my ass from a camp of cannies. If it wasn't for Henry, I'd be on a spit with a damn apple in my mouth." He took a step in front of Henry so if Ben fired, he would end up riddling Lyle first with bullets.

"Doesn't matter, Lyle. The town charter says anyone that comes into our town has to give up their weapons. It's the law," Ben declared flatly.

Henry rolled his eyes, as if he had seen this coming. That black and white line was a solid as ever. He knew Ben wasn't going to give in so he nodded to Jimmy, and gestured to the pickup truck.

Henry glanced to Lyle and said, "Look, this was a mistake. I think we'll just get back in our truck and head on out. Thanks anyway, Lyle. We'll be seein' ya." He took a step back and all weapons turned to him. Henry looked up to see the muzzles of the guards guns now trained on his chest. He frowned, though his Glock was pointed at them in turn.

"What, you're gonna shoot me right here in the road? And for what? For not wanting to obey your rules? Well, take this into consideration. One man squeezes a trigger and there's gonna be blood spilt on both sides of that wall."

Lyle looked up at Ben, his arms wide as he pleaded for the security chief to give in.

"Ben, come on, man, this isn't necessary, they're friendly. Let 'em in the town with their guns. I totally vouch for them, they're good people."

Ben eyed Henry who glared back in return, neither man breaking their gaze. All it would take is one guard, or one of the companions to see something they didn't like, didn't trust, and lead would fly, killing more of them than anyone cared to admit.

Finally, after the longest minute recorded on the planet, Ben lowered his gun and told his men to do the same.

"All right dammit, fine, Lyle, they can come in. But if one thing happens, it's on your head," he warned him.

Lyle nodded, understanding completely. "I get it, Ben, everything'll be fine, trust me." He tried to smile for reassurance but it fell flat.

Ben backed away from the wall and a second later a large portion began to slide to the side. It was on large steel tracks, and despite its size and appearance, moved like it was on ice. The tracks were greased and the gate barely made a sound.

Ben appeared on the ground now and he stepped through the gate. Henry walked over to the man and they stared each other in the face, no more than two feet separating one another. Ben was a few inches taller than Henry, but Henry's upper torso was wider, more muscular. Still, if the two men had been in a bar brawl, the odds could have gone either way.

"The pickup stays here. We'll take it inside for you," Ben told Henry as he stared at the gore-covered vehicle.

"What the hell for?" Jimmy asked as he stepped closer.

"No one drives in town but my police force and the mayor. Those are the rules of this town; take it or leave it." His eyes creased and Henry saw this was something the companions wouldn't get, so he decided to let it go. They had their weapons and that was good enough.

"That's fine, Ben, we can walk. Jimmy, give him the keys," Henry said.

With a moan, Jimmy tossed Ben the keys. He caught them while still looking at Henry. The two stood like two kids in the playground, each deciding the other was king of the schoolyard.

"Anything else?" Henry asked with a grin.

"Yeah, there is. I run a tight ship, fuck up and I'll see you hanging from a rope. You got me?"

"Yeah, I got you; you won't have any trouble from us, Ben. We just want to rest up and then we'll be on our way. Oh, and you've seemed to have forgotten something. We were invited here after saving your man Lyle from the stew pot. A little gratitude would be appreciated." He turned to Cindy, Mary and the others and waved them on, then pointed to Lyle to join him.

Everyone did as they were told and Henry, with his group, stepped through the gate and into the town.

As Lyle passed Ben, he grinned again. "Don't worry, Ben, nothing is gonna happen, I promise."

Ben nodded curtly as he turned and followed them into the gate. He tossed another man the truck keys so he could fetch the pickup.

"Hmm, well see," Ben said, "We'll just see."

The man who caught the keys jumped into the pickup, started it, and drove it through the gate.

The sides scraped lightly on the sides of the tight opening but the paint was far from mint.

With the pickup inside, the gate slowly slid closed, sealing off the outside world, and perhaps trapping anyone in the town inside, as well.

Chapter 13

Lyle caught up to the companions as they walked down the road leading into town, taking their time and enjoying the day.

The actual town was within sight and was barely a quarter mile from where the cement wall had been built. As they walked, Lyle filled them in on the lay of the land and what they could expect from the townspeople.

"What about trouble?" Henry asked. "You got any troublemakers with a chip on their shoulder?" Henry asked Lyle as they strolled down the road. Cindy was limping slightly but her ankle was doing well, and Jimmy was hovering over her like a hawk.

Sue and Raven walked at the rear, talking quietly together and Mary was walking by herself a few feet to the right of them.

"Yeah, we got a few," Lyle responded. "But it's mostly some of the sec guards wanting to blow off some steam after their watches on the wall. They're usually at the local bar. We only have one bar now. Once we're all barricaded into the town, space was precious and the other bars in town were converted to stores and such."

"What's the story with that Ben guy?" Jimmy asked. "He seems like a real hardass."

Lyle glanced over his shoulder to Jimmy and nodded slightly. "I suppose he is, but when the rains came and people turned into zombies, we all had to make some hard choices around here. After the police chief got killed by a bunch of dead ones, Ben stepped in and took charge. He and the mayor got things on track, organized the town and got us to build the wall that's kept us safe for almost two years now. Without Ben, I don't want to think what might have come of this place."

Henry nodded, understanding completely. He'd heard it a hundred times. When most people went running for the hills, there were always a few strong men and women who took charge, knowing what needed to be done. Ben sounded like one of them. But Henry still figured he didn't want to get on the wrong side of the man. There would be no latitude if Ben thought Henry or one of his group had done something wrong.

"What about the deaders?" Jimmy asked. "I didn't see any out by the wall, the last one we ran over was almost a half mile away."

Lyle glanced back at Jimmy again. As he did this, he snuck a glimpse at Mary but when she returned it, he looked away and back to Jimmy. She had made it clear what she wanted and he would respect her.

"They come and go," Lyle told Jimmy. "Sometimes a dozen'll show up and sometimes it's just three or four. Since the wall's been built, they don't pose much of a threat to the town."

"So it's safe here?" Cindy said as she hobbled behind Jimmy.

Lyle nodded. "Pretty much. We've had some trouble with raiders now and then. They have a place a few miles from here. They set up shop in an old Ford factory. The place is surrounded by chain-link and razor wire, and the fence is like, twelve feet high. From what I hear, they have a good thing there, only they won't be friendly. Shit, just last week they managed to hit one of our search parties. They killed the lead man and took the women hostage. They do this all the time. Sooner or later the women accept their new fate and become one of them."

Henry slowed and looked Lyle in the face. "Wait a second. You mean to tell me raiders have some of your people and you haven't gone to get them back? Why the hell not?"

Lyle shrugged. "Simple, we don't have the weapons or manpower to penetrate their base. That building was where Ford built their cars. It's huge, made out of concrete and steel." He shrugged. "My sister was taken in the last raid and I sure as hell want to get her back, but it's suicide to try."

Mary walked up to Lyle and touched his arm. "Oh, Lyle, I'm so sorry. Your sister? That's terrible."

Jimmy spit in the dirt and shrugged as he raised his shotgun. "Fuck, Lyle, if it was my sister they took, I'd have gone in there blastin' and to hell with what might happen. Shit, she'd be my sister."

Lyle's face took on a look of pain as he pointed a finger at Jimmy. "Don't you think I know that, Jimmy? Hell, if I thought I had even the slightest chance I'd take it, but there's no way. They have over thirty men and women and they're armed to the teeth. There's just no way. She's gone. If she's not dead then she's as good as. I've learned to accept it and I don't see why the hell you shouldn't either. Now come on, it's getting' late. If you want to get a meal we need to be at the bar by five. That's where all the food is served to people who live in town, that is unless they live somewhere with a kitchen, and you guys will get put up in the small motel we got at the north side of town. And they don't have a kitchen."

He turned and walked away, not caring if they followed or not.

Henry looked to Jimmy and the others and frowned. "So much for a place of safety," he said.

Without waiting for a reply, Henry followed Lyle, picking up his pace so the clean-shaven man wouldn't outdistance him.

Chapter 14

Lyle turned left at the first street once he'd entered town and led the companions through the winding streets, eventually slowing and pointing to a brick building with the word, **_Johnny's_** above the door. As they moved closer, the companions could see the word Johnny's was made out of neon bulbs, though now the bulbs weren't on.

As they approached the door and Lyle opened it, the sounds of people talking, laughing, and music wafted out.

Jimmy turned to Henry and said, "You think it's a mistake to go into one of these places, Henry?"

"Why's that?" Henry asked him.

"Well, it seems every damn time we go into a bar there's trouble. If we just stay the hell out of them maybe we could avoid some trouble once in a while."

Henry smiled widely and chuckled. "But, Jimmy, where would the fun be in that? Come on, just keep your nose clean and we'll be fine."

Cindy pushed past Jimmy and mumbled, "Pussy," as she entered the bar. She was joking but the message was clear to Jimmy. Shut up and go inside like the rest of them. Mary, Sue and Raven were next.

Henry followed with a sly grin, thinking of what Jimmy had said. The younger man had a point but then, this was where all the lowlifes and troublemakers hung out. And truth be told, if someone was gonna fuck with you, they would do it irregardless of where you were. The trick was to be ready and have the upper hand when it happened, because Henry knew it usually would. It was the way of the world nowadays and in many ways it always had been, even before the dead began to walk.

There was a short hallway leading into the actual bar and to the right of the doorway was a wooden plaque with the words, ***LOOSE LIPS SINK SHIPS*** inscribed. But the latter two words were crossed out and replaced by the words: ***WILL GET YOU DEAD***.

The rest of the picture showed a torpedo hitting a United States warship, the entire plaque harking back to World War 2. Still, the meaning was clear. Have a big mouth and you might get a loaded gun shoved into it.

Henry was the first of the companions to enter the bar after Lyle. The instant he set foot, he creased his eyes to let them adjust to the darkness. Oil lanterns hung from the ceiling and were on tables, a heavy cloud of smoke filling the room. It was the same everywhere, no matter what year it was. A bar was a bar, with loud music, raucous laughter and the smell of cigarette smoke.

More than one table had men and women playing poker and blackjack. If it wasn't for the country music and the modern clothes the patrons wore, the bar would have looked like the set of an old cowboy movie.

Lyle gestured to a table in the middle of the room and Henry shook his head no. He scanned the room and spotted a booth in the far corner and he pointed to the table. Lyle, shrugging, led them to the table Henry picked.

Jimmy said nothing, knowing what Henry was doing. The corner table allowed the companions to have their backs to the wall and thus see anyone coming at them. In the middle of the room, they could do no such thing. Much like an outlaw in the Wild West, if you got lazy you would get dead before you knew it had happened.

As they sat down, a waitress came over and said hello to Lyle. "Sorry about your sister, Lyle. Sharon was a great girl," the waitress said.

"Thanks, Mandy, I miss her, too," Lyle responded.

"So what'll it be?" Mandy asked.

"Beers all around, honey," Lyle said and glanced to Henry to make sure it was fine. Henry nodded it was. "And whatever the special is, too, one for each of us."

Mandy wrote the orders down on a notepad. "Okay, beers and pork sandwiches, coming up," she said.

Jimmy looked at Lyle, his eyebrows going up in surprise. "Did she say pork?"

Lyle nodded. "It's canned pork, but it's not bad."

Jimmy's face sagged. "Oh, I was hoping for the real thing."

"Sorry, Jimmy," Lyle said. "Not many pigs out here in Colorado. Thank God for all the canned goods we find on our search parties. Oh, and we're growing our own food, too, of course."

Jimmy leaned back in his chair. "Of course," he added.

Mary nudged Cindy and used her chin to point to a table of young men in their twenties sitting across the bar. "Hey, Cindy, looks like you got yourself a fan club," Mary grinned.

Cindy looked where Mary was pointing and sure enough, there were four men sitting at a table, all staring at her and talking together. When she made eye contact with one of the men, he waved to her. Being polite, she waved back and the men all began to laugh like a bunch of little girls.

"Ignore them," Lyle told Cindy. "They're harmless."

"Who are they?" Cindy asked.

"They're all on the city's parole as workers. They fix the roads and keep the buildings maintained. City workers. All except the one on the left; the one with blonde hair. That's Max, he's Ben's son."

"You'd think they never saw a woman before," Henry said as he eyed the men for possible trouble.

"Well, not like Cindy," Lyle said. "We have attractive women here but as you already know, Cindy is a knockout." He looked to Cindy. "I didn't mean nothin' by that, Cindy, just stating a fact."

Cindy smiled. "Not at all, Lyle, and thanks for the compliment."

Jimmy pulled Cindy close and kissed her on the cheek. "And she's all mine," he grinned and she pushed him away with a chuckle.

"And Mary is equally gorgeous," Lyle said as he smiled at her. Mary nodded politely and when she knew no one else was looking, she flashed Lyle an angry look. He turned away, regretting what he'd said. She'd already made it clear on her position, though he'd hoped she may have had second thoughts.

It was at that moment that Mandy arrived with beers and sandwiches, distracting the companions who were hungry and thirsty.

As they dug into their meals, none of them caught the look of Ben's son when he saw Jimmy kiss Cindy. The man's jaw grew hard and jealousy flitted across his face. Resting on his knees, his hands curled into fists.

He was used to getting what he wanted in Cement City, as his father was the security chief, and as he stared at the companions and Cindy most of all, he decided he wanted her for himself and he could care less if she was with Jimmy or not.

Chapter 15

The companions and Lyle spent the next hour relaxing after a good meal. Mary, Sue, Raven and Cindy were talking while Lyle filled Jimmy and Henry in one more time about the town.

Cindy decided she needed to use the bathroom and Mary agreed to go with her. Jimmy held on to her M16 and the two ladies headed off to the bathroom.

As they went, Ben's son, Max, watched the two women crossing the bar to the women's room.

It was when they disappeared into the bathroom that Max nudged three of his buddies and they each stood up and went to the small hallway that led to the bathrooms. Though there was no running water, buckets were set up next to large barrels similar to oil drums. It was simple to use the water to flush the toilets with. The water wasn't running in the pipes but the sewer systems relied on gravity and a simple pouring of a bucket into a toilet flushed it easily.

It was as Mary and Cindy exited the bathroom that they found themselves blocked by Max and his three buddies.

"Well, hello there, ladies, allow me to introduce myself. I'm Max, my father runs this town with the mayor."

Mary looked at Max and his buddies and nodded curtly. "I'm sure you're very proud of him, now if you'll excuse us, we want to get back to our friends."

"Please, don't let us stop you," Max said as he slid to the side to allow Mary and Cindy to leave. Mary went first but no sooner was she past them then the men closed the gap, trapping Cindy between them.

"Hey, what's the big idea?" Cindy asked as she stared at Max.

"Nothing, baby, I just thought we could get to know one another a little better." He reached out and brushed a wild curl off her forehead, but Cindy slapped his hand away like it was a hot poker.

Max's face grew hard. "That wasn't very nice, bitch, I'm tryin' to be nice here. There's a lot of women in this town that would love to have me give them my attention."

Cindy took a step forward, not afraid of Max in the least. "Then go see one of them, 'cause I'm not interested." She glanced down at his groin. "And even if I was, it doesn't look like you're packin' enough to make it worth while."

This caused a titter of laughs from the other men and Max's face grew red. He was being insulted by this woman and now she was making him look foolish in front of his men. That he couldn't allow.

"You just chose to say no to the wrong man, bitch," Max growled and reached out to grab Cindy by the hair. But as his hand went to her head, she reached up with her right arm and blocked the hand at the wrist, then she punched Max in the stomach with her free hand.

Max exhaled hard as the blow knocked the wind out of him. Cindy's punch felt like a mule had kicked him, partly because she had angled it to nail him in his solar plexus. Max saw stars as he leaned over and wheezed.

Cindy wasn't through with him yet and she used her right knee, bringing it up and connecting with Max's forehead, sending him up and backward where one of his men caught him.

While this was happening, Mary had dashed back to their table, wanting to let the others know what was going on. Henry looked up from chatting with Lyle to see a concerned look on her face.

"Henry, we got trouble," she said and pointed to the hallway leading to the bathrooms.

Jimmy followed where Mary was pointing, and when he saw Cindy in a fight with Max, he was the first up, his shotgun in his hand as he dashed across the bar, shoving anyone in his way out of his path.

He arrived just as Max was recovering from the blow to his forehead by Cindy's knee.

"Why you little bitch, you'll pay for that with blood," Max growled and pulled a knife. Cindy's eyes went wide and she tried to back away, realizing this simple bar brawl had just been taken to the next level. She could see the hate in Max's eyes and knew he was telling the truth. He wanted blood and it would be all hers.

But then Jimmy was among them. He used the butt of the shotgun to club the first of Max's goons in the back of the head. Like a sack of potatoes, the man went down—he didn't move again.

Swinging the shotgun around, Jimmy used it like a bat, the stock connecting with the next man's chin. There was a loud *crack* and the man went flying off to the side to land on a corner table with a shattered jaw. There was a cacophony of yells as he flattened the table and drinks and food went flying. This started a fight amongst the occupants of the table and soon six people were brawling. Jimmy was still moving and he never saw what he'd started. With his left foot, he kicked the last man in the balls, feeling testicles deflate like spent balloons. The man's scream of pain went up in pitch and he crumpled to the floor in a fetal position. He wouldn't be making babies ever again.

That left Max, who had time to prepare himself for Jimmy's attack. When Jimmy came at him, Max grabbed a nearby chair and swung it, knocking the shotgun out of Jimmy's hands. The weapon clattered across the floor to be lost under shifting feet.

By now the bar was a mass of fighting, screaming people, a wave of violence that consumed everything in its path. Henry, Sue, Raven, Lyle and Mary found themselves in a battle for their lives as people who didn't know them now came at them with fire in their eyes.

A man came at Raven and she picked up a beer bottle and smashed it over his head. The man dropped to the floor, unconscious as glass rained down around him. Henry saw this and was glad she was showing restraint. If she used her razor sharp fingernails here and killed someone, it wouldn't bode well for any of them.

Jimmy had recovered from losing his shotgun but Max was quicker. The man came at him with a hunting knife, slashing back and forth like a cage fighter. Jimmy backed away as Max moved forward.

A fighting pair of patrons got between the two men and for a second Jimmy lost eye contact. But then the fighters were past and Jimmy spotted Max just as the man came at him from the right. The knife flashed by his eyes and only instinct prevented him from being blinded.

Then Jimmy went on the attack. Kicking out with his right boot, he knocked the blade out of Max's hand but the man wasn't giving up, and he charged at Jimmy, wrapping his arms around him as the two combatants fell to the floor, rolling about.

All around them, men and women screamed and battled as the bar fight sucked in everyone inside it, a massive black hole of violence that swallowed everything and began to grow with each second.

Max got his hands around Jimmy's neck and began to squeeze. Jimmy tried to break the hold but Max was slightly larger than him and knew how to use his superior weight and strength. Jimmy felt the world going hazy as his oxygen was cut off.

Then something bumped his head and he reached his right hand over and tried to grab whatever it was. His finger wrapped around the hilt of Max's knife. Someone had kicked it back to him across the floor with their foot.

With his vision growing dim, and the other companions caught up in battles of their own, Jimmy knew he only had himself to rely on.

With no other choice, he brought the knife around and slammed it into Max's throat, the blade slicing into the flesh easily only to erupt out the other side, the hilt now flush with Max's neck.

Max's grip on Jimmy's throat immediately loosened as the man began to spasm, blood shooting out of the wound to bathe the floor red.

A pair of brawlers that were close enough stopped in mid-punch when they saw Max on top of Jimmy with a blade sticking out of his neck. Soon others were doing the same as the entire bar watched as Max fell over and began to twitch while his blood seeped out to pool on the floor.

By the time Max died, his eyes still open but seeing nothing, the bar was silent, no one speaking or moving. Max was well known by the entire town and to see him dead was unthinkable. No one would dare kill the security chief's son. Not if they wanted to keep breathing afterward.

Cindy pushed people aside and ran to Jimmy, hugging him and helping him to his feet.

"I'm okay, baby, I'm fine, he's the one who got what's coming to him," Jimmy said as Cindy hugged her man.

All eyes were on Max's corpse, and then one at a time, each patron turned and stared at Jimmy, as if he had committed the most heinous act imaginable.

Then, one of the patrons closest to Jimmy raised his hand and pointed at Jimmy and yelled, "Holy shit, he just killed Max!"

"Fuck me, he did," another man said. "Get him!"

And before Jimmy or the rest of the companions could move, Jimmy and Cindy found themselves swallowed by an avalanche of bodies as the bar patrons turned their wrath on Jimmy for killing one of their own.

Chapter 16

Jimmy and Cindy were surrounded by men and women, each wanting blood for the death of Max. Jimmy felt repeated blows to his face and lower body and he pulled Cindy under him, protecting her from the worst of the abuse. He couldn't breathe as feet kicked him repeatedly and he knew it would only be a matter of time before someone struck a vital organ.

So when a loud gunshot, followed by another one, filled the bar, stopping the beating, at first he didn't think it was real, that it was just his ears ringing from the battering his head was taking.

But then he heard a loud voice yelling out through the bar.

"What the fuck is going on in here? Get the hell off those two people, goddamn it."

Almost immediately, the beating stopped and the patrons of the bar dispersed. Jimmy waited a second, not wanting to raise his head from between his arms for fear he would be struck, but when no more blows fell on him and Cindy, he risked a peek.

He saw Ben standing in the bar doorway, four of his men behind him, the guards all with firearms leveled at the patrons.

At first Ben was staring at the patrons, not knowing what was going on, but then his eyes shifted to the left and suddenly went wide when he recognized the clothing of his fallen son.

"Max?" was all he said as he ran to his boy and dropped to his knees. As he picked up his son and cradled the still form in his arms, he looked at the hilt of the knife jutting from his neck. The blood was congealing now, the heart no longer pumping. Tears formed in the corners of Ben's eyes as he gazed down on the face of his dead son. He reached out and gently closed Max's eyelids, at least now he wouldn't have to stare into his son's dead eyes. Ben stayed like this for a full minute, rocking his son back and forth as he fought to control his grief. Then he carefully set the body down and stood up, picking up his rifle as he did so.

"Who did this? What the fuck happened here?" Ben demanded in a cold voice. "So help me God, if someone doesn't tell me who killed my son, I'm gonna..."

That was all he had to say. Like one perfectly harmonious group, all fingers went to Jimmy, no one speaking, scared of what might happen to them if Ben heard a voice.

Ben followed the pointing fingers to Jimmy and he covered the six feet separating them in three strides. Without hesitation, he placed the muzzle of his rifle to the back of Jimmy's neck and cocked the weapon.

"You give me one fucking reason why I don't pull the trigger and end your miserable life right now, you piece of shit," Ben growled as he pushed the muzzle deeper into Jimmy's flesh.

"I'll give you seventeen," Henry said in a hard voice as he placed the muzzle of his Glock against the left side of Ben's head, just behind his ear. "You pull that trigger, friend, and your brains are gonna mix with his. Now what do you say we all calm down and talk about this. This is one hell of a misunderstanding."

"I don't think so," Ben said. "Men?"

Two dozen metallic clicks—the sound of weapons being readied—filled the bar as Henry looked left and right to see everyone in the room aiming a handgun at him, Mary, Cindy and the others of his group. Even if he shot Ben, the rest of the companions were as good as dead.

"Checkmate, fucker, now take that fucking gun away from me before I decide to take my chances and see to it that you and your asshole friends are sent straight to Hell," Ben hissed, not the least bit intimidated that he had a gun pressed to his head.

Henry considered his options, his eyes peering into each of the men and women who now held him at gunpoint. Though he hated to do it, he knew Ben had him cold.

Pulling back the Glock, he lowered the weapon, his jaw tight in anger at seeing his bluff called, and then squashed so easily.

Ben turned to four men and a woman and got their attention, then he pointed to Jimmy.

"You, five, get this piece of shit up and take him to the podium. We're gonna do this fucker right. He's gonna hang for what he did to my son. And someone go get the mayor, he needs to be there, too. We're gonna do this nice and legal."

Immediately a cheer went up as Jimmy was dragged away by gunpoint and the rest of the patrons found out there was going to be a hanging.

One of the guards Ben came in with stepped up to him. "What about the rest of that guy's people? What do you want to do with them?"

Ben turned to look at Mary, Cindy and the rest of the companions who were still being watched at gunpoint.

"Take them to the podium, too. If I find out they had anything to do with my son's death, they're all gonna swing." He gestured to the companions' weapons, especially their knives. "And take their guns and blades from them."

The companions were quickly disarmed. With muzzles to their backs, they were told to go outside. While they were pushed out of the bar, Henry caught a glimpse of Ben getting a tablecloth to cover his son. He felt sorry for the man, as he had just lost his son, but not so sorry that he wanted to give his life so the man would feel better.

As the group was marched through the streets, more people were coming out of the buildings, all eager to see a hanging as word spread like wildfire.

"Looks like we're the talk of the town," Henry said to Sue as they were herded like cattle down the middle of the street, his smile trying to reassure her that he would see her safe before it was over.

"Shut the fuck up, asshole," a guard said to Henry and to make sure Henry understood, he poked him in the back with the muzzle of the rifle. With a grunt, Henry turned and glared at the man, but he remained silent. Though his visage looked calm, he was wracking his brain for a way to get them free and make an escape, but so far nothing came to mind.

At the podium, Henry and the women were told to stop when they reached the ladder leading up to it. Jimmy was already there, having been taken from the bar a few minutes earlier.

Henry moved next to Jimmy and shook his head in anger. "Christ, Jimmy, we've been here for less than two hours and you've already got us about to be hanged. You're getting better as you get older."

"But Henry, it wasn't my fault. That fucker I killed back there was gonna kill Cindy. I had no choice."

"He's right, Henry, that asshole came at me with a knife," Cindy said.

"Forget it already, it doesn't matter how we got here. What we need to do now is figure out how to get out of it before we all have to wear scarves on our necks to hide the marks of our hanging," Henry told them.

"All of you, shut the fuck up!" one of the guards demanded, smacking Jimmy in the back of the head with his rifle as he stared at the companions. They all stopped talking, not wanting to receive a whack in the head like Jimmy, who was wincing from the pain. A small trickle of blood seeped down into his shirt collar now, thanks to the guard's gunsight cutting into his scalp.

The crowd was getting bigger all the time, more and more people arriving to see the hanging. The sun beat down on the six companions' heads, making them weak from thirst.

Finally Jimmy moved next to Henry and said, "What the hell is taking them so long?"

Henry turned slightly so he was looking Jimmy in the face. "Are you serious? Don't be an idiot. You want them to hurry up and hang you? Shit, Jimmy, you can't be that stupid. The longer they take the better our chances are. Now shut up and look innocent."

Henry glanced at Sue and his heart broke at the fear on her face. "Be strong, Sue, I promise you this isn't gonna happen."

She smiled wanly. "I'm going to keep you to that promise." Tears were rolling down her cheeks.

"I think I can get away," Raven said as she studied the men guarding her. They weren't close enough to hear her speak, as they had moved away a few feet to talk.

"No, Raven, not yet," Henry said. "No wild escapes until we know we have no choice."

"Then when?"

"Don't worry, you'll know," Henry said flatly.

"Hey, someone's coming down the middle of the street," Mary said. All eyes went to where she was looking. They saw a pudgy man in a top hat waddling down the center of the road.

A few voices muttered the man's name and Henry knew right away he was looking at the mayor of the town. This fat, balding man was Mayor Bigelow.

The mayor was quickly joined by Ben, the two talking heatedly until Bigelow glanced at the companions. He was frowning as he did so and Henry shook his head.

"Damn it. That doesn't look good. I don't wanna know what Ben is telling that man," Henry said.

"This is all a big mistake, Henry," Jimmy tried to defend himself yet again. "That guy's son tried to kill Cindy. I had to save her."

Henry glanced to Jimmy again. "Jimmy, I already told you, it doesn't matter what happened. All that matters is what that guy thinks happened." Henry gestured to the mayor who was waving his hands in the air at Ben.

"All of you shut the fuck up or there won't be any need of a hanging," the guard closest said as he aimed his rifle at the companions. Henry shut up, not wanting a whack to the head. He had already figured the odds of what would happen if he spun, kicked the guard behind him in the balls, and took the man's gun.

But what then? He might shoot one or two other guards before they knew what was going on, but by then the rest would fire on him and his people. And though Raven and the others of his group could handle themselves, Sue was a liability. She wouldn't go into combat mode if he and the others tried to escape. And he wouldn't leave her either.

No, they were trapped, outgunned and surrounded. If he was going to get them out of this, it was going to be with his mind, not his brawn.

"Hey look, he's coming this way," Cindy said and all eyes went to the mayor, who was waddling his way to the podium. He passed the companions with barely a glance and pulled his heaving bulk onto the podium. He was now looking down on his people, who were clapping and cheering for their leader.

"What the hell does that fat slob have that has these people loving him so much?" Jimmy had to ask as he looked to his right at the mayor.

"Who cares," Henry snapped. "The only thing that matters is that guy believing you're innocent, and the rest of us, too. Or else we're all gonna need new shirts 'cause the ones we have now aren't gonna fit our necks anymore."

Henry turned to Mary, nudging her to get her attention. "Mary, see if you can get Lyle's attention, maybe he can help us out. He saw what happened at the bar; maybe he can talk some sense into Ben."

"I've already been trying to, but so far he won't look at me," she said.

"Well, try again," he told her.

Mary did what Henry said and she called out to Lyle. One of the guards was going to hit Mary in the back with his gun but Henry stepped forward and shoved the man off balance. He missed her but Henry got a blow to the shoulder blades by another man for his trouble.

"Try that again, stranger and it'll be a bullet you'll feel," the guard warned Henry.

"Understood," Henry said as he rubbed his back with his hand, wincing. There would be a bruise there he knew, one of many to add to the collection.

But Mary's cry worked and this time Lyle looked at her. Mary waved for him to approach and he did. She was thanking God she had slept with him last night. Hopefully the bond they had shared would come in handy now.

When Lyle reached the companions, a guard stopped him but Lyle shoved past the man.

"Get out of the way, Fred, I want to talk to the woman."

"But Ben said..."

"I don't care what Ben said. Move out of the way," Lyle snapped.

Cowed, the man shifted to let Lyle pass. All the while, on the podium above, the mayor was talking about justice and how a terrible loss had befallen the town. Ben stood by his side, nodding at his words. Every now and then Ben would glance to the bottom of the podium at the companions, his eyes falling hard on Jimmy. The man wanted justice and revenge, but at the moment they were intermingled.

"Mary, I'm so sorry for all of this," Lyle told her.

"Then do something, Lyle. Get us out of this mess. You know damn well Jimmy didn't murder that man's son. It was self defense."

Lyle shook his head. "There's nothing I can do. Ben wants justice and he's the sec chief for Christ's sake."

Cindy spoke up. "But I can attest to what happened. That guy came at me and Jimmy was only helping. If Max hadn't pulled a knife on me, none of this would have happened. He would still be alive."

Lyle shrugged helplessly. "No one's gonna believe you, Cindy. You're Jimmy's girlfriend. Yeah, I saw the way Max was eyeing you but no one will listen. I tried to talk to Ben already."

While Lyle and the women were talking, Henry had been concentrating on a way out of their predicament. His brain was working overtime as he struggled to come up with an angle, something that was worth not killing Jimmy and perhaps letting them all go free. But what would be worth their lives?

And then he had it. He had a bargaining chip that the mayor, Ben and the rest of the town might find worth letting them live, if just for a little while longer.

"Hey, Lyle," Henry called to him. "Come over here, I have an idea I want to share with you."

Lyle stepped closer to Henry, the guards around them getting itchy with their guns.

Henry glanced at the closest man and smiled. "Easy there, Tex, we're just talking here, don't get trigger happy."

The guard said nothing and Lyle moved closer. "Yeah?"

Henry leaned in so only Lyle could hear him. "I have an idea that might just get us a reprieve, but you need to go and suggest it to the mayor. See what he thinks." Henry told Lyle his plan and the man's eyes, once relaxed, slowly went wide with surprise. He soon became more than a little excited at what Henry was proposing.

When Henry was finished, Lyle turned to Henry and looked him square in the face. "You're kidding; you'd do that for me? For the town? But it's suicide."

Henry waved his arms around to encompass their situation. "At the moment it's the better bet, don't you think? It's worth the risk and if it works out we get to leave with no strings attached. So go tell him and see what he thinks about it."

Lyle nodded, glanced at Mary with a smile, and climbed the podium to Ben and the mayor, who stopped talking and began to confer while the townspeople began to talk amongst themselves, not understanding what was going on. Many cast furtive glances at the companions, more than one of them wanting blood.

The companions all turned their heads to look at Henry in curiosity.

"What did you tell Lyle?" Cindy asked.

"Yeah, Henry," Jimmy said. "What's the big plan?"

"Let's just wait and see what happens, guys. If the mayor or Ben won't go for it, then it doesn't matter anyway."

The companions all turned and looked up at the podium to see Lyle arguing with both men. Ben didn't look happy about what was being said, but the mayor kept nodding, a sly smile on his lips. He liked what Lyle was saying and Henry was beginning to have hope that his idea was working.

Finally, the talking was over and Ben tuned and marched away and off the podium. As he passed Jimmy, he stopped and stuck his finger in Jimmy's chest.

"This isn't over, you fucking bastard. I'll see you swinging soon enough. And if I can't, then a raider's bullet to your head will have to suffice." He stormed off, leaving Jimmy to wonder what just happened.

The mayor walked to the edge of the podium and held his arms up so the people would quiet down.

"Ladies and gentlemen, please, listen to me. There have been some new developments and at this time, there will be no hanging!" the mayor said grandly.

The crowd began to moan and complain as the mayor raised his hands again. "Wait, wait, listen to me, please! I have good news! Lyle has informed me the outlanders, feeling guilt for what has happened, will risk a rescue on the raiders' camp to save our captured people. If they're successful, they will bring our people home."

"And what if they don't?" a voice cried out from the crowd.

"Then the raiders will kill them in ways that would make hanging seem merciful. This is better, people. At least our loved ones now lost might have a chance to be returned to us."

"But what'll stop them from just leaving? They could keep on going once they leave the town!" another voice cried, causing others to add their voices to the mix.

The mayor nodded, acting like a stern mentor. "That will be taken care of as well. Each of them will be fitted with an explosive on their ankle. If they try to leave or don't return at the designated time, we can manually detonate the explosives and kill them easily. We have nothing to lose here and all to gain." He paused for a moment as he looked into the eyes of his people. "So, are you with me?"

Some of the crowd dissented but more than ninety percent agreed. Then the rest joined in, falling to the majority. Soon, the crowd was cheering as the hopes of getting back loved ones became a reality.

While they cheered, the companions all turned and looked at Henry, scowls on their faces for what he'd volunteered them for—namely a suicide mission.

"What?" Henry said. "Would you rather be hanging from up there?" He pointed to the nooses. "At least now we've got a chance."

His four friends stared at him and then each one relaxed and let go of their anger, realizing he had a point. On the podium above, the mayor was dispersing the crowd who were wandering off, a few still glancing at the companions as these were the people who wanted to see a hanging.

The mayor waddled down off the podium and stopped in front of the companions. He was dripping sweat and looked like a pig in a suit. The man gestured to one of the guards. "Bring them to the police station, and keep them under guard. Then get Chris to get the leg bands ready. I want them leaving at first light."

"Yes, sir," the guard said and ran off.

Mayor Bigelow turned to look at Henry and the others. "You six may have done a terrible thing in killing Max, but the act you're about to perform is mighty noble. We'll talk later after you're fitted with your leg bands. Until then, you'll be escorted to a holding cell at the police station. I'll be along later to fill you in on what you'll be doing."

He turned and walked away, waddling back and forth like a duck.

The guards made the companions move out, and as the sun hung in a cloudless sky, they were marched to jail to await their leg bands full of explosives.

"Hey, guys, look on the bright side," Jimmy said as they walked down the middle of the street, people staring and pointing at the prisoners, more than a few whispering about what they were going to do and how.

"Jimmy, what the hell could possibly be good about what's happening to us?" Henry asked.

Jimmy shrugged. "Well, at least we're not dead yet."

No one could argue with his reasoning, though what the next day would bring was another thing entirely.

On the roof of a store that used to sell cell phones, a crow cawed at the six travelers, as if it knew something of the future they didn't.

Chapter 17

Later that night, the companions had a visitor in their jail cells.

A middle-aged man by the name of Chris came in carrying a small wicker basket filled with electronic wire, metal bracelets, and other odds and ends you might see an electrician carrying.

Ben had gone home for the night and to see to his son's funeral. The entire time he'd stood watch over the companions, Henry had expected the man to pull his gun and shoot them dead, despite the deal the mayor had worked out with them. But the man had restrained himself, for the good of the town, he'd told them.

Another man was on watch this night. He was tall, well over six feet, with a beer belly that would make him fit right in with the freaks at the local circus. He was a smart man, too. He made sure to only open one cell at a time and to never get close enough to the cell bars where one of the companions could get the drop on him. Earlier, he had taken down the companions' names, threatening them if they didn't give their true identities. Henry decided it didn't matter and had told everyone to be honest.

Henry was first to receive his ankle bracelet full of C-4. When it was locked on his leg, a small red light came on, telling Henry the bracelet was armed.

Chris said nothing the entire time, nor did he explain anything about the ankle bracelets. When Henry tried to prod the man for information, he simply said, "Ben will explain it to you in the morning, don't you worry about it."

Henry still prodded the man some more but it was for nothing.

An hour later, each of the companions was wearing an ankle bracelet on their right leg, one that was as strong as a single handcuff.

As Chris left, his job done, he did offer one piece of advice. "Oh, and I wouldn't try and mess with those bracelets if I were you," he told the six travelers. "There's a sensor in each one, and if it's tampered with it'll go off."

"And what happens then?" Jimmy had asked.

Chris had smiled slightly. "Well, if it does go off, there won't be enough of you left to bury in a shoebox." He'd waved and departed then, leaving the six friends to think about his words.

The rest of the night was uneventful and Henry advised them all to grab some sleep. The next day was going to be a hard one and they should take what rest they could.

Late in the night, while the six friends slept, Ben returned to check in on them.

As Jimmy slept with a slight smile on his face, Ben had stared at the young man through the iron bars, his right hand caressing the butt of his gun.

Despite the mayor's deal, it took all of his will not to shoot Jimmy as he lay sleeping, wanting vengeance for what happened to his son.

Jimmy, not knowing how close to death he was, slept on in blissful ignorance.

Chapter 18

With the sun just touching the sky, the six companions were roused from their beds and dragged out of their jail cells by gunpoint. For breakfast, each of them was tossed a sandwich made from stale bread and peanut butter. Not looking a gift horse in the mouth; each had eaten the poor breakfast quietly, knowing it was better than nothing.

Surrounded by five guards with guns cocked and ready, the friends were led to the main gate, where the mayor, Ben and a few other men and women of importance waited patiently.

The mayor walked up to Henry and nodded politely, as if they were two men meeting on a street corner for lunch.

"Good day to you, Mr. Watson. So, are you still onboard with what was discussed yesterday?"

Henry stared the man down, his eyes cold. "Don't see why not. Not much of a choice. But you better live up to your end of the deal, Mayor. I'll tell you that right now."

The mayor nodded politely as if Henry had stated that it looked like rain. "We honor our deals here, sir. You save our people and you will be allowed to go free. You have my word on that."

Jimmy spit in the dirt, scowling. "Well, Mayor, your word doesn't mean much, as none of us know you from shit."

The mayor blinked at Jimmy, but if he was going to become angry, he held it in.

"Then I guess you're going to have to trust me." His eyes creased and his face darkened. "You don't have a choice in the matter, you know."

"We need our weapons back," Henry said simply, wanting to change the subject.

The mayor nodded. "And you will get them back, Mr. Watson, but first there will be a little demonstration to show you how serious we are about you not deciding to try and run away. You see, I don't trust you either. That's what the bracelets are for. Call it an incentive to complete your mission and return here with our captured people." He gestured to the gate leading out to the road and Henry and the others began to walk with him, the guards right behind them. Henry had never stopped searching for a way to escape, but until he knew more about the bracelets they all wore, he decided it was better to wait. He told the others as much and they had agreed.

"I don't like this, Henry," Mary said as she moved up next to him.

"Me neither, but they have us cold. Look, just stay quiet and toe the line, once we're out of this damn town we can figure out how to get the bracelets off and hightail it to the next state."

She nodded and fell back to Cindy and Sue to share what Henry had said.

Jimmy moved closer to Henry and gestured to the gate with his chin. "This is fucked up, Henry. I can't believe we have to do this."

"Well, we do, Jimmy, so please, just keep your mouth shut and listen for once."

Jimmy opened his mouth to reply but Henry held his hand up. "Starting now," Henry told him coldly.

Jimmy closed his mouth and nodded, deferring to Henry.

Upon reaching the gate, Ben waved the companions on to the wall so they could get a good seat for the demonstration. On the opposite end of the gate, the mayor and other townspeople were gathered. The mayor and others were holding umbrellas, and though the sun was going to be strong today, Henry didn't understand why the people felt the need to use an umbrella. It wasn't *that* hot out.

Ben said nothing as way of a greeting as Henry and the others gathered on the wall, but he did point out onto the road so that the friends could see what was so interesting.

"What the…?" Henry said as he looked out about a hundred feet from the main gate. Beside him, Jimmy, Mary, Sue, Raven and Cindy said the same thing in different ways.

Off the shoulder of the road, chained to a large steel post that was once used for a streetlight, were two zombies.

They were nothing special at first glance. Their clothing was filthy and disheveled, their visages gaunt and pale, one or more features missing by either rotting off or being torn off. One was male and one was female. Other than that, Henry couldn't tell what they may have looked like back when they were alive and breathing.

Henry glanced to Ben who raised his right hand to stop Henry from asking unwanted questions. "Just watch the two dead ones and it will all be made clear. Especially watch their necks and heads."

Henry did as he was told and he now split his attention between Ben and the two ghouls.

Ben reached into his pocket with his left hand and came out with two small, black boxes. The boxes fit easily into the palm of his hand and consisted of a small antenna on the top and a simple red button, which was covered with a plastic casing. The plastic had to be flipped open first if a person wanted to press the button. On the side were four more buttons, each with a number on it. These resembled a small bicycle lock.

"This one is for you and your friends, this other one is for those two zombies out there," Ben informed Henry and the others as he pocketed the box designated for the companions. "To disarm the box a code had to be manually punched into the numbers on the side. Only I know the code and can set you free. Remember that if you have any ideas about coming back to the town and killing me in my sleep instead of going to the raiders' camp." He held the black box up for all to see. "Observe," Ben said and gestured to the two zombies. He flipped the plastic covering up, then pressed the red button.

Henry and the rest of the group, as well as the mayor and his entourage, all turned to watch the zombies below.

A second after Ben pressed the button, there was a loud explosion and the two zombies were vaporized. It was as if a massive blender had come down out of the sky to land on the zombies, instantly pulping them to a mist of bone matter and gore.

Up on the wall, everyone was peppered with zombie bits and Henry realized what the umbrellas were for. Each umbrella was open and protected the mayor and his entourage from being pelted with blood and gore.

For almost a minute, bloody debris rained down, then it stopped, only a pink mist floating on the breeze to mark where the zombies were. Well, that and a large crater three feet deep and seven feet in diameter.

"And that's half of what you guys have in your bracelets, Watson," Ben said in a maniacal tone. "Just in case you think I'm bluffing, know this. If I even think you're running, I'll press the button for your bracelets and send you all to Hell on the wind. You got me?"

Henry glanced to his friends, who nodded back. Each had bits of red and brown on their face from the wind blowing blood splatter on them, but their eyes were hard and their jaws set. They knew the score and were with him.

"Yeah, I think we got the message loud and clear," Henry said. "So if you're done posturing; where are our weapons? If you want us to actually succeed in saving your people, we need to have our weapons back."

"And you will have them," Ben said. He turned and waved to a set of guards waiting below near the gate. "Go down and get them, those two have them."

Henry led the way with the others following, and in a minute they were back on the ground. Up on the wall, the mayor watched with creased eyes, letting Ben handle the matter of outfitting the companions for the rescue mission.

Henry was first to reach the two guards and he noticed the men carried a black duffel bag between them, each man holding one of the cloth handles.

"You boys have something for us?" Henry asked.

Neither man said a word, only tossed the heavy duffel bag at Henry's feet.

Henry bent over and unzipped the bag, his heart skipping a beat to see his Glock and panga on top of the rest of the groups' armaments.

"Jimmy, give me a hand here, will you, please?" Henry asked, and as the younger man moved in to help, Henry passed him the guns and knives for the others.

Five minutes later, the six friends were armed and ready to leave.

Ben walked up to them, as he had been watching silently from a few feet away, and he tossed them another duffel bag.

"What's in there?" Henry asked as Raven moved to investigate.

"Water, food, some spare ammo. Whether I like it or not, you work for us now, and if you're mission is to succeed, you need supplies."

"Hey, Henry, there's a couple of hand grenades in here," Raven said as she held them up, careful of the locking pins.

"That's right. I figure you're gonna need them to get inside that factory. They're set up pretty good there. It'll be a miracle if you manage to save anyone, let alone yourselves."

Cindy frowned and crossed her arms. "Thanks for the vote of confidence."

Ben glanced at her. "Wasn't doin' nothin' of the kind. Though I would hate to see any of our people die that might be saved, I'll sleep just fine if you all never make it out of there alive."

"Forgive us if we do our best to disappoint you," Mary said as she checked her .38. It seemed fine; no one had messed with it.

"That's why I'm coming, too," Lyle said as he walked up to the companions, a backpack on his left shoulder, a Parker twelve-gauge double barrel shotgun on his right, and an assault rifle in his hand. On his hip was a small automatic pistol, the grip worn from use as well as a seven inch hunting knife.

"Lyle," Ben said with wide eyes. "What the hell do you think you're doing?"

Lyle stepped closer to Ben so he was between Henry and him. "I'm going with them, that's what. You forget, Ben, my sister is one of those people you spoke about and I'm gonna do whatever it takes to get her back. I told you before, these are good people and if they're going to try and save my sister, then as a man I have to be there, too."

Ben glared at Lyle, the two locking gazes, but eventually Ben looked away. Throwing up his hands, he began to turn away. "Hey, it's your funeral, go, but when they shoot you in the back or I send them all to Hell in pieces, don't blame me."

Lyle smirked slightly, a wide one that cut across his face like a dagger. "Wouldn't think of it, Ben." He took a step after him. "But listen, about your son, I truly am sorry. It was a terrible accident."

Ben spun on Lyle, his gaze shifting from him to Jimmy. "That's bullshit. That outsider killed my boy and if it was up to me, he'd have a neck size too big for his shirt right now. So don't tempt me 'cause even the mayor can only stop my vengeance for so long." He waved to his men. "Come on, boys, we're through here." When he was ten feet away, he paused and looked back at Henry and friends. "Lyle knows the way to the factory, at least now I don't have to worry about you getting lost." Then he continued on, leaving Henry to watch him, only three guards with weapons on them remaining. Henry watched Ben go, knowing there was no need for the man to watch the companions or have his men do so. All he has to do was press his red button and they were all dead.

Mary stepped closer to Lyle. "You don't have to come with us, Lyle, really."

He turned to her and gazed into her eyes, lost in the deep blue color of them. She looked so beautiful and all he wanted to do was kiss her.

"Yes, Mary, I do. I wasn't lying about my sister and I want to make sure you get through this in one piece," he told her.

"I can take care of myself, Lyle, and I've done so since long before I met you," she replied.

"You two okay?" Henry asked as they prepared to move out.

Mary turned to him and nodded. "Fine, Henry, me and Lyle were just talking about his sister."

Henry stepped up to Lyle and slapped him on the shoulder. "Thanks for coming, Lyle. Don't worry, if there's a chance in hell of saving her, then goddammit we'll find it."

"That's what I'm hoping for," Lyle replied. "Now come on, follow me. Once we get down the road a bit I know where we can get some transportation."

"You do?" Jimmy asked. "You mean we're not gonna have to hoof it all the way to the factory?"

Lyle nodded. "Yup, there's a small gas station about a mile down the road. In the back, mixed in with the other old heaps, is a working pickup truck similar to the one you guys had. We keep it there for emergencies."

"What happened to our vehicle anyway?" Henry asked.

Lyle shrugged. "Don't know. If it was salvageable, then it probably ended up in our fleet of cars and trucks. If not, then they took it apart to use for spare parts. Either way, consider it gone. Call it paying taxes, I guess."

"Shit, the fucking end of the world and I'm still paying taxes," Jimmy said. "Talk about irony."

They had begun walking, crossing through the gate and leaving the wall behind. The mayor was talking loudly to his people, telling them about the grand rescue attempt. Neither Henry nor the others listened or cared for his pomposity.

"You know, Lyle," Henry said. "Even if we manage to save your sister and the rest of the captured townspeople, unless we figure out a way to get these bracelets off, Ben is gonna press that button no matter what."

Lyle glanced at him. "Yeah, I was thinking the same thing. But hopefully there will be something in the factory we can use to get those off you without blowing you all up."

Mary chuckled. "Yes, that would be nice."

"I feel like a criminal," Sue added as she walked beside Henry. Raven said nothing, stoic as ever.

"Tell me about it," Cindy added. "If this thing on my leg goes off, I think I'm going to have a really bad hair day."

Jimmy moved up next to Cindy and gave her a hug. "Aww, baby, you'd look good even if you were bald."

She laughed. "Oh, really? Well, I just might take you up on that one day. These locks don't comb themselves, you know."

Mary and Sue laughed too, knowing what Cindy meant. In the world of the dead, hair care was slightly more difficult than before.

Despite their predicament, the companions were in high spirits. They had learned long ago to take each day as a gift, and to hell with tomorrow.

If there was a way out of their situation, they would find it.

The rest would be left to fate.

Chapter 19

Now that they were out of the town, the walking dead were everywhere. More than a score had to be put down in the one mile walk to the gas station.

Henry had taken down half on his own, using his panga, and Jimmy and Lyle had taken care of the rest, using the stock of their shotguns to crush in heads and shatter jaws.

The seven people slowed their gait as they came in sight of the gas station.

Henry was in the lead and he had his Glock out, his eyes studying the dilapidated building. There were two gas pumps on the side, both nozzles now lying in the dirt, the underground tanks long dry. There was no weather port built to protect the patrons as they filled up their gas tanks, the entire area exposed to the elements.

The building itself was falling apart after two years of neglect. All the windows were broken and missing, shards of glass littering the dirt and the door was hanging off, only the top hinge still holding it upright, and only barely. From Henry's perspective, one good breeze would have the door off the frame and on the ground. Weeds grew all around the building, in many places covering the walls, and more than one spot had vines burrowing into the mortar of the foundation. Another few years and the structure would be buried in foliage.

"Looks cozy," Jimmy commented as he moved up next to Henry.

"Yeah, well, we aren't staying so it doesn't matter," Henry replied. "Let's get the pickup Lyle said is here and get moving." He gazed up at the sun, now high in the sky. "I want to get to the factory before it gets dark, then I want to do a recce. And later, if all goes right, we'll hit the raiders just after dinner or what I hope will be their dinner." He turned and pointed to Sue, Cindy and Raven. "You three stay out front and keep an eye out while the rest of us go get the pickup truck."

"Sure, Henry, no problem, I could use a break," Cindy said. Her ankle was feeling better but it still pained her to walk. It had been a hard mile for her and she relished getting to sit down once more and ride instead of walk.

"I want to come with you," Raven said.

Henry shook his head. "Not this time, Raven. Just stay here and watch our backs."

"Fine," she said, not feeling like debating for a change, though she was pouting.

Henry waved for Lyle, Jimmy and Mary to follow him, and they headed to the rear of the gas station.

Once Henry peered around the corner to see it was clear, he let Lyle lead the way as the man knew which vehicle they wanted.

The lot was huge, with junk cars filling a quarter of a square block. Most had no tires, especially the ones further back, but the ones closest to the gas station seemed to be in better shape. More than one had busted windows and headlights that were missing, the gaping holes like eye sockets without the eyes.

"This way, it should be in this corner," Lyle said as he led the way.

They followed him, one eye watching the old cars for signs of trouble at all times. It was a maze of metal and steel and anything could be hiding in the rows of old junk.

"Oh great, we got deaders," Mary said as she stopped walking and raised her .38.

The others paused and looked where she was pointing.

Sure enough, weaving their way through the junk, were five zombies. Three were male and the other two were female, each in different states of decay. One of the males was all but a skeleton, while one of the women looked like she had died and returned that very same day.

Mary was about to shoot, as was Jimmy, when Henry placed his hands on their shoulders and stopped them both.

"Wait, guys, don't shoot. All it'll take is one gunshot and we'll have every deader in the area on top of us. Look, there's only five of them and four of us. We can take them easily in hand-to-hand."

"How do you want to do it?" Mary asked as she studied the approaching ghouls.

Henry took a step away from them and pointed to a pile of plumbing pipes on the ground.

"There's plenty of junk around here we can use for weapons. Grab something and choose your targets," Henry said as he picked up a brake drum and hefted it. "No one needs to get within four feet of them."

Jimmy went to the pile and picked up a steel pipe about two inches round and five feet long. He waved it back and forth like a spear. "Hey, Henry's right, this will work great. Okay, let's get those fuckers."

"Don't get cocky, Jimmy," Henry snapped. "This isn't a game."

"Yeah, yeah, old man, I know it's not," Jimmy replied as he moved through the rusted and dented cars to take out his chosen target. One of the male zombies was three cars over and it turned off to head for him while the others continued towards Henry, Mary and Lyle.

Jimmy climbed onto the hood of a beat-up Buick Skylark, and when the ghoul was right below him, he rammed the pipe into the center of its face.

The pipe went in easily, sliding through the sinus cavity and then into the brain. Jimmy put so much force behind it that the tip of the pipe punched through the back of the zombie's skull, causing it to hang on the pipe as Jimmy held the body upright, the zombie spasming and thrashing as whatever had animated it now fled the rotting corpse.

He only held the ghoul like this for a few seconds, then he let go, not wanting the weight of the body to pull him off the car.

The pipe clattered against the front fender as it dropped, and the zombie went to its knees to then fell over, the pipe preventing it from lying prone when it became wedged between the bumper of a station wagon. Dark brain matter spilled from the tip of the pipe like rotting porridge, thanks to being scooped out as the pipe exited the skull. Jimmy wiped his hands in a clapping motion and jumped off the Buick to see if anyone else needed help. But it seemed clear that the others had their chosen ghouls well in hand. With nothing else to do, he leaned against the rear fender of a Cadillac and watched the show.

The second male ghoul had chosen Henry for its target and the warrior found he was now the hunted. But he wasn't some frightened victim. He was a man who had killed more ghouls than he could count, and one more was barely worth thinking about.

As the zombie came for him, assuming Henry would be easy prey, the deadlands warrior used the brake drum as an airborne bludgeon. He threw it at the zombie as hard as he could, the rusted disc flying across the seven feet separating them in less than a second. The drum hit the ghoul in the chest so hard half a dozen ribs were cracked, but as the drum fell to the ground, the zombie was unfazed by its wounds.

Stumbling back from the blow, it quickly regained its balance and renewed the attack.

And Henry was ready for it. As the ghoul came at him, Henry smoothly pulled his panga from its oiled sheath and took a step to his right, much like a bullfighter would do when the bull approached.

The zombie, not able to turn fast enough thanks to its dull reflexes, found itself passing Henry, who pivoted on his heel, raised the panga high in the air, and brought it down in a chopping motion.

The head was severed from the neck in one smooth blow, the head falling straight down where the zombie's feet kicked it a few times as it continued walking forward. Then the body went limp and dropped forward, hitting the ground in a puff of dust.

The head remained active, the eyes flicking back and forth, the mouth opening and closing, as the dried lips and tongue attempted to moan.

Henry kicked the head under an old van and forgot about it, his attention on any new danger. He saw Mary and was about to go help her, but he saw she had things well in hand.

One of the female zombies had decided Mary was a worthy victim and had broken off from the others to come for her, a low moan emanating from its cracked lips. As the ghoul stumbled through the row of cars, Mary picked up an off-white, concrete block a foot long.

It was hollow in the middle and used for building foundations, and how it ended up in the back of the gas station was a mystery. But the block served Mary well for what she had in mind.

The zombie wore a business power suit, once gray, but now a dark black thanks to all the dirt, grime and blood covering it. The skirt was torn, showing the once shapely legs of the ghoul, and the stockings it had worn were long shredded and missing.

As the ghoul moved within a few feet of Mary, she was ready for it. Lifting the concrete block overhead like a weightlifter, she threw it at the zombie with as much force as she could muster. The block soared through the air and the left corner impacted with the ghoul's forehead.

There was a meaty *thwack* when stone met dead flesh, and the zombie's head nearly cracked in two from the blow. The block sent the dead woman flying backwards to land hard on its back.

But though seriously wounded, the brain was still intact, and no sooner did it fall then the dead woman was trying to sit up. As its head turned to the left and was about to rise, Mary's combat boot came down hard on the face, the heel of her foot crushing the head and allowing brains to spill out like pudding in a squished plastic bag.

She twisted her heel back and forth for a moment, applying more pressure, and as the arms dropped back to the ground, she pulled her boot away, using the zombie's ripped skirt to clean the sole of her boot. Smiling at herself for her ingenuity, she turned to see how the others were doing.

Jimmy was leaning against a car and Henry was also standing still, and he nodded to her when they made eye contact.

When she turned to the right to see where Lyle was, she saw he was just about to take on two zombies at once. But before she could go and help, she watched as he attacked the two ghouls, using more discarded auto parts as weapons.

Lyle didn't mind having to deal with two zombies while the others had only one each. He knew he could handle it easily and on top of that, he wanted to impress Mary.

As the skeleton-like zombie and the dead woman who looked fresh came for him, his eyes quickly darted to the ground to see what he could use as a weapon.

A radiator fan blade with one of the five blades missing caught his attention and he reached down and pulled it out from under the car it was lying beneath. The fan blade was rusted and dented but would serve him well.

As the two ghouls came around a beat-up Chevy Vega, and were in a direct path with him, he waited for them to move closer.

The male zombie took the lead, looking for all purposes like a scarecrow, the few tatters of clothing hanging off it in rags. When the ghoul was no more than six feet away, Lyle stretched back the arm holding the fan blade, and threw it at the ghoul like it was a Frisbee.

There was a low humming sound as the fan blade arced through the air, wobbling slightly thanks to the missing blade, and a second later, one of the blades on the fan had imbedded itself in the zombie's face right between the eyes.

As for the ghoul, it stumbled about, not understanding why its vision had become so skewed.

It tripped and went head first into the bumper of a Pontiac, and the force of the landing pushed the fan blade deeper into its head, slicing its brain in two and killing it almost instantly.

That left only the dead woman coming for Lyle. He stood his ground, watching her shamble toward him like a drunken woman at last call. Her eyes were glassy and her mouth hung slack, but even in death she was attractive.

Her blonde hair hung in loose curls, and if a man could get past the maggots crawling in her hair or the cockroach that peeked out of her left ear, then she was still quite a catch.

His eyes scanned the ground once more and found a bent tire iron near the rear tire of a black Firebird with an eagle painted on the hood. Grabbing it, he prepared himself to take down the last ghoul.

She was only a few feet away, and Lyle still hadn't raised his weapon. It was something in the dead woman's face that made him hesitate. She looked so alive, though dazed, but alive nonetheless.

He only paused for a heartbeat, but it was enough for the dead woman to get close enough to attack him.

As Lyle stood dumbfounded, he saw the teeth of the dead woman coming for him, ready to take a chunk out of his neck. He noticed idly that the teeth were unusually white for a zombie.

Chapter 20

Henry was too far away to help Lyle when he saw the man falter in his battle with the woman zombie.

From his vantage point, it seemed as if the man had decided on a change of heart at the last moment, as if he couldn't make himself kill the ghoul.

As Henry pulled his Glock free of its holster and tried to line up the dead woman's head in his sights, he already knew he would be too late to stop it from biting Lyle.

Lyle stumbled away from the ghoul, his heels tripping over some scattered junk behind him, and he found himself falling backwards. As he fell, the dead woman was following, already lunging for his neck.

As Lyle hit the ground, the back of his head struck pavement and he saw stars. As he blinked his eyes clear, he saw the open mouth of the dead woman as she prepared to sink her polished teeth into his throat.

Then, as if it was happening in slow motion, Lyle saw an object swing in from out of his peripheral vision and connect with the dead woman's head. The head was knocked to the side where it was stopped by a car.

The object that had struck the head continued moving and crushed the head against the side of the car, the skull cracking and brains shooting out in all directions.

The zombie was now very dead and its arms and legs twitched as whatever had brought it back from the dead now returned it there.

Lyle blinked up at the shadow over him, and for a moment thought it was another zombie, which would take the place of the former. But as his vision cleared, he saw it was Mary.

She was standing over him, a dented and rusty steel rim from a Volkswagen still in her hand. She had used it as a bludgeon and had slammed it so hard into the zombie it had cracked its head like an egg.

With the rim dripping brain matter, she tossed it away. It bounced off the hood of a car and rolled in a circle, like a giant coin that wouldn't go down. Finally, it stopped and quiet descended over the rear lot.

"You okay?" she asked as she reached for him to help him up.

"Thanks, I don't know what came over me," he said, standing up.

"It's fine. Sometimes when they look too human it gets hard. It happens."

"Yeah, I guess that's what it was. Still, thanks."

They made eye contact and something passed between them, something from the other night when they had been intimate. Then the spell was broken as

Henry yelled, "Hey, you two, let's get going, daylights wasting."

They smiled bashfully, turned away like two teenagers on a first date, and walked to join Henry and Jimmy who were now waiting for them.

"Good to see you made it through whatever just happened over there," Henry said curtly.

"Yeah, Lyle, and it was a good thing Mary was there to save your ass," Jimmy quipped. "Or it would be you lying between those cars."

"Jimmy, stop it," Mary snapped.

"No, Mary," Lyle said. "He's right. You saved my butt. I froze."

"It doesn't matter what happened," Henry said. "It's over and done with. Now stop worrying about what ifs and point out the pickup we can use."

Lyle pointed to a dark-blue, five passenger Toyota pickup with chrome wheels, ultra thin tires that were only a few inches off the ground, and a yellow stripe down both front fenders. "There it is. That's the one."

"Damn, what Spanish guy did you steal this from?" Jimmy asked as he strolled over to it, looking like a guy hanging out at a car show on a Friday night. He walked over to the pickup and reached for the driver's door handle. He was talking about what a vehicle like the pickup would look like out on the street, the woofers shaking the frame and everything around it as Macarena blasted out of the speakers, and he was so busy cracking jokes that he didn't check inside the pickup before opening it.

Pulling the door open, he never saw the zombie hiding in the backseat, that is not until it popped up and lunged for him with its mouth open wide and hands clawing at his face.

Caught entirely off guard, Jimmy only had time for a, "What the fuck?"

Then the ghoul was on him, and he knew his time on the earth was over.

Chapter 21

The smell of decay and rot was overwhelming to Jimmy's senses, and he found himself tasting bile as he fought off the attacking ghoul. His arms were out at his sides, and his shotgun went under his body as he fell to the ground.

The zombie moaned loudly and reared its head back, ready to snap it forward like a striking Cobra. Jimmy knew he had seconds to live.

But then, just behind the zombie, a shadow blocked out the sun and Jimmy saw something silver flash overhead.

There was a slicing sound and Jimmy realized where the zombie's head should have been there was now only open air. And then he felt the wetness as pus and congealed blood soaked into his shirt from the jagged neck wound that was the stump of the zombie's former head.

Blinking his terror away, Jimmy pushed off the body and bucked his hips to get himself free. Mary was there a moment later and she helped pull the corpse off him.

"Holy shit, that was close. Thanks, Henry," Jimmy said as he stood up. Henry was standing over the headless body with his panga in his right hand, the blade dripping gore.

"What did I tell you about being careless, Jimmy? If you'd checked inside the cab before opening the door, you wouldn't have almost got your nose bit off."

"You're right, Henry, I'm sorry," Jimmy said apologetically.

"And further more, if you had...wait, what?" Henry said, not believing what he'd heard Jimmy say. He expected to hear a lot of wisecracks and sarcastic remarks, not an admission of guilt.

"I said you're right. I fucked up. I'm just glad you had my back."

"Oh, well that's good to hear for a change."

Mary stepped between the two men and smiled widely as she said, "If you two women are done, we should get moving, no?"

"Huh? Oh, sure, Mary, absolutely. Jimmy just broke character and I don't know how to feel about that," Henry replied.

Jimmy flashed Henry his famous shit-eating grin. "What can I say? I'm a complex guy." He looked down at his shirt and made a disgusted face. "What do I do about this shit? Ah, damn it smells." His shirt was covered in gore and a translucent slime. More than two dozen maggots squirmed about in the viscous fluid.

It was Lyle that solved the problem as he searched inside the pickup's cab for the ignition key. He found it under the mat, just where he knew it was supposed to be. Reaching into the back seat, he pulled out a colorful Hawaiian shirt, complete with pineapples.

"Here, wear this," Lyle said and tossed the shirt to Jimmy.

"Thanks, man, I guess there's no accounting for taste, but then I don't have much of a choice, do I."

"No, you don't," Henry said flatly. He looked at Mary and said, "Honey, go tell Sue, Cindy and Raven we're all set and will be right there."

"Okay, Henry," she said and with a smile at Jimmy while he changed shirts, she headed off to the front of the gas station.

Henry turned to look at the pickup when Lyle started the engine. It turned over on the second try, and after sputtering for a few seconds, it evened out.

Henry slapped Jimmy on the back, the Hawaiian shirt making him look like a convention attendee.

"That's a good look for you, Jimmy. It's good to know when the raiders are looking for a target to shoot, you're gonna stick out like a sore thumb," Henry joked. "You'll be the first thing they aim at, which means my ass will be safe."

Jimmy frowned but didn't say anything. He had already resolved to find a new shirt at the first possible opportunity.

"You guys comin' or what?" Lyle asked from the driver's seat.

"Yeah, we're coming," Henry said and he and Jimmy climbed into the rear bed. There was room for five of them in the cab, but he wanted to be out in the open, in case there was trouble.

Lyle swung the pickup out of its parking spot and drove to the front of the gas station. As the pickup left the rear lot, the rear tire drove over the headless corpse, snapping bones and allowing more pus and gore to squirt out and stick to the rear tire well.

The women were waiting for them and Sue waved at Henry when she saw him.

Henry could see the worried look on her face and knew Mary had been filling in Raven, Sue and Cindy on the situation with zombies they had come across in the rear lot.

As Lyle stopped in front of them with a soft squeal of brakes, they each climbed into the cab, Mary and Sue handing Henry the packs with supplies in them, including the grenades.

When everyone was situated in the cab, Henry looked at Jimmy beside him, the younger man nodding, his jaw firm, his eyes hard.

Henry slapped the roof of the pickup and called out, "Okay, Lyle, let's go get your sister!"

Lyle replied by stepping on the gas pedal, the truck surging forward, leaving a spray of gravel and dust behind it. He swung onto the road and sped off.

The raiders' camp was only a few miles away, and they would be there shortly.

Chapter 22

The seven people stood on the hill overlooking the Ford factory.

"Well, I was wondering why we hadn't seen any deaders. I guess there's my answer," Henry said as he gazed down at the factory below.

"No shit," Jimmy added softly.

"There's so many of them," Mary said from beside Jimmy.

"How the hell are we supposed to get in there?" Cindy asked, shifting from her bad foot to her good foot.

"No wonder my people never tried to rescue anyone taken, it's impossible," Lyle said in despair.

Below them, surrounding the factory was a twelve foot high chain-link fence. But that wasn't what was so imposing. It was the hundreds of zombies gathered around the fence like teenagers trying to get into a rock concert.

Five and ten bodies thick, they were pressing on the fence, their hands shaking the links as they fought to enter the factory perimeter.

Their moans were so loud nothing else could be heard and to simply see so many zombies in one place was frightening.

The walking dead knew the factory was full of human beings and they wanted the fresh meat desperately. As long as they believed there was food inside, they would never leave.

Henry used his binoculars to study the layout of the factory. There was a large rollup door to the right and a smaller door for pedestrian traffic to the left of it. This door was used regularly as he watched raiders come and go. There were two raiders on guard at the moment, both leaning against the building as they smoked cigarettes. If they seemed intimidated that they were surrounded by zombies, they gave no inclination. Each one carried an assault rifle over their shoulder and both wore sidearms. One wore his sidearm in a holster while the other had his jammed into the front of his pants. Henry wondered if the man was smart enough to have the safety on. If not, and he wasn't careful, he would be singing in a slightly higher pitch before long.

There was a parking lot with vehicles in it off to the left of the building. A Land Rover, three Jeeps, a few hatchbacks, a Cadillac and a Mustang, to name a few, plus the regular pickup trucks like Dodge F-150s and Rams. There were also a couple of Custom Harley Davidsons, as well as a few rice rockets, the two different machines looking at odds parked next to one another. There was also a city transit bus.

"If we run into a bind, we can hotwire one of the older cars and use it to escape. And if things go well, we can all get on that transit bus with the prisoners and drive back to Cement City in style," Henry said.

"So you're really going back to town?" Lyle asked Henry as he stared at the horde of zombies in awe. He'd never seen so many in one place at one time.

Henry shrugged. "Don't see as we have a choice, Lyle. Once Ben knows this 'op' is done and we've saved your people, he promised to take these off us." He shook his leg to refer to the ankle bracelet.

"I don't trust that guy farther than I can throw him," Jimmy said. "And I can't throw for shit."

Henry patted Jimmy's arm. "One problem at a time, Jimmy. But I have to agree with you on that one, though. Still, we can't worry about it now. First let's save some people, then we'll deal with Ben."

There was a soft sound of footfalls from behind them and everyone turned abruptly with guns drawn, only Henry not moving. He knew who it was before she arrived as he was the one who sent her out on a recce to the other side of the factory.

Raven appeared from out of the foliage and smiled when she saw everyone pointing their guns at her. "Was it something I said?" she joked.

"Jesus, Raven, you need to alert us a little more before you pop up," Jimmy said. "That's a good way to get yourself shot."

"What did you find?" Henry asked her, ignoring Jimmy.

Raven slid up beside Henry and nodded to the zombies below.

"One side has no deaders. It's a good place to sneak in. And there's a few trees too close to the fence. We can climb them and hop right over."

"Seems sloppy leaving the trees like that," Jimmy said.

Raven shrugged. "Maybe, but it's been two years since anyone trimmed the trees and deaders can't climb. I don't think they're worried about intruders jumping over the fence, either."

"Good point," Jimmy agreed.

"Is that how we're going to get inside?" Sue asked beside Henry.

He turned to her and placed his hands on her shoulders. "That's how we are, but not you."

"What? Why?"

"Isn't it obvious by now, Sue?" Henry said. "It's not gonna be safe in there and I can't be worrying about you. I need to know you're safe. So we're going in but you're staying out here with these." He handed her the binoculars. "Any deaders come towards you I want you to climb one of these trees." He waved his hand around them. "When we get back and find you in a tree, trapped, we'll take out the deaders and all leave, safe and sound."

"But, Henry..." she began.

He placed his index finger on her lips, then took it away and kissed her. "Please don't argue, I want to know you're safe. Is that so bad?" He whispered so only she could hear him.

"No, I guess not."

"Good, now that that's settled, we need a distraction so the raiders won't know we're sneaking in," Henry said as he turned to face the others. "We need a diversion so loud and attention grabbing that when it happens, they'll be far too busy dealing with it to bother with us. So, anyone have any ideas?"

No one did and they stood around for the next fifteen minutes, each having at least one idea that Henry quickly shot down.

Jimmy had the most ideas, though each one was more hare-brained than the last. He suggested everything from cutting down trees and rolling them, to driving around with the pickup, blaring the horn to draw the zombies away.

But the last one jarred an idea in Henry's mind, and while Jimmy and the others debated this and that, he worked out his plan in his head.

He didn't think Lyle was going to like it much, but the more he considered it, the more he thought it was the only feasible way to cause a large enough distraction to fill their needs.

"Okay, people, I have an idea that should work," Henry said. "Here's what we're going to do as soon as it get's dark."

Chapter 23

The cloudless sky allowed a half moon to bathe the factory in pale moonlight. Other than a few torches set up around the factory, all was wreathed in shadow and blackness.

The moan of the dead continued unrelenting, though the raiders had grown accustomed to it, accepting that their lair would always attract the living dead.

Two raiders stood watch near the door leading into the building. These two men were almost identical to the two Henry had spotted. Both carried automatic weapons and both smoked cigarettes. Their hair was unkempt and their body odor was a tad overripe.

As the two men chatted about who they would be fucking that night from the stable of female prisoners, the first raider looked up at what he thought was the sound of an engine.

It was hard to know for sure, as he had to separate the noise from that of the moaning dead, but as he listened a little harder, he heard the distinct sound of a racing engine.

Turning away from the second man, the raider walked away from the building, his eyes searching the hillside outside the fence.

And then he saw twin lights hovering a few feet off the ground, and they were coming straight for the fence and the crowd of zombies.

It took him a few seconds to let his eyes grow accustomed to the night once he left the perimeter of the torchlight, and when they were adjusted, he spotted the distinct outline of a pickup truck barreling down the hill, going fast and picking up speed with each yard traveled.

The first thing he thought was the driver must be crazy. As soon as the pickup struck the crowd of zombies, it would be bogged down by the corpses. Even if it reached the fence, it wouldn't matter as the momentum would have been lost and the heavy duty chain-link would prevent it from going any further.

"Hey, Mac, have a look at this. Some idiot's trying to attack us," he joked as he waved his partner over to him. The same zombie horde that was a threat was also a deterrent. It was an undead moat that prevented attack from all but the most foolish and stupid.

The man called Mac walked the distance separating him from the other man and both stood and watched the pickup as it flew down the hill, bouncing and jumping as it covered the rough terrain.

But as the pickup reached the first ghouls, what both men expected to happen didn't. The pickup didn't begin to lose speed until it finally stopped, only to then have the driver pulled from the cab and devoured by the hungry dead.

Instead, the pickup plowed into the zombie horde until it was almost to the fence, and as it was jolted to a halt, the pickup suddenly erupted in a blazing fireball that sent bodies flying off in all directions.

The blast wave was enough to send the engine surging out of the front of the vehicle, to hit the fence and knock down a section of it. As the flaming truck pieces rained down across the area, the two raiders' mouths fell open as the first of the ghouls that were unscathed began to pour into the breached perimeter.

The dead had finally been allowed access to the factory...and they were hungry.

Five minutes ago.

"Okay, so we're all set to send this baby down the hill," Henry said as he finished jury-rigging the pickup truck, turning it into a rolling bomb.

"You really think this will work?" Lyle asked as the others stood nearby, preparing themselves for the battle to come.

"Sure it will," Henry said to Lyle. "Here, let me go over this one more time." He pointed to the grenade jammed in the back of the engine by the air filter. The pin was still in it. "This one doesn't need the pin pulled. When the other one goes off it will set this one off, too." He gently closed the hood and moved around so he was pointing into the driver's seat. Inside there was a another grenade with the pin removed. The grenade was situated so that the handle was jammed between the seats, thereby keeping the handle engaged.

There was a small piece of string tied to the handle and the other end of the string was tied to a fist-sized rock. The rock sat on the seat, looking like someone had forgotten to take their pet rock with them after leaving the vehicle.

"Okay, Lyle, pay attention 'cause I'm only going through this once. See the rock tied to the grenade?" Lyle nodded he did. "Good. When the pickup plows into the first deaders and is jarred to a halt, kinetic energy will do the rest and the rock will go flying to the front of the cab. When this happens, it will pull the grenade out of the seat, the handle will pop open, and boom, we have ourselves a distraction."

He carefully reached inside, turned on the engine, and then hit the switch for the headlights, wanting to add some flair to the plan. Then with a stick about as thick as his thumb that Jimmy had cut to length, he jammed it between the gas pedal and the seat.

"Okay, here goes nothin'," Henry said. He reached in and yanked hard on the transmission shifter, then jumped back as the pickup truck surged forward and began rolling down the hill, the engine roaring as the floored gas pedal pushed it onward. Henry was hit on the shoulder by the doorframe as he jumped out and he fell to the ground, but he was up a second later, dusting himself off. He mentally chastised himself for getting slower in his old age.

All the companions and Lyle gathered together to watch the pickup truck roll down the hill.

It bounced and jounced and eventually hit the zombie horde, but then nothing happened.

Jimmy chuckled. "Great, old man, it looks like your plan didn't go off as..." And then the night was filled with light, fire and noise as the grenades went off one after the other, followed by the pickup's gas tank, which was a quarter full. Jimmy took a step back as the flaming debris went soaring off in all directions, despite the fact that he was perfectly safe so far up the hill.

Henry nodded, proud of his idea and glad to see it worked perfectly. But there was no time to gloat or study his handiwork.

"Okay, people, let's get moving, we've got people to save." He kissed Sue in passing and she watched her five friends and Lyle melt into the foliage, to soon be gone from sight.

With nothing else to do, she gripped her .22 more tightly and watched the inferno below, as the bodies burned and the first of the undead horde began to enter the perimeter of the factory.

Chapter 24

It didn't take the companions and Lyle long to climb the trees bordering the chain-link fence and jump over it. Once everyone was down, they quickly made their way to the back of the factory. There were many windows with metal mesh integrated into the glass and a multitude of metal doors. Henry, Jimmy and Lyle went from door to door, finding them all locked and when finished, they gathered in the center to discuss what to do next.

Jimmy spoke up first with a wave of his shotgun. "We can shoot our way inside. Blow the lock off one of the doors and get this shindig going."

"Shindig?" Henry asked, amused at his friend's choice of words.

"Yeah, why, you never used that saying before?"

"No, I have, it's just...never mind."

"Okay then, shoot our way in it is," Jimmy said and leveled his shotgun at the closest door. This door hadn't been checked by any of them and Jimmy assumed it was locked like the rest. He was about to fire when Mary rested her hand on Jimmy's arm and said, "Wait a second, will you, please? God, always shooting and worrying about the consequences later." She took a step to the door and turned the doorknob, then smiled smugly when the metal door popped open

"Well hell, Mary, I could have done that," Jimmy said sarcastically.

"Then why didn't you?" she asked.

"Never mind, you two," Henry said, seeing a squabble coming if he didn't stop it. The two were like brother and sister, always looking for a chance to needle the other.

The sounds of destruction carried around the building and a suffuse glow of orange and red could be seen. The zombies were now inside the perimeter, and if the companions didn't get in and out fast, they would find themselves dealing with the undead as well as the raiders.

"Okay, I've got point," Henry said, his tone saying there would be no discussion on the subject. "Then Jimmy, Lyle and the girls follow me in that order. Stay sharp, this is where it gets serious."

Henry entered the building, seeing nothing but darkness. As he let his eyes adjust, he saw he was in a massive room filled with the remnants of an assembly line. Old machinery, steel carts, sagging metal arms for machines, gurneys, belts and assorted tools were scattered everywhere. Looking left and right, he saw the doors he was checking outside were clearly visible from the inside as well.

The large wall had a metal door every twenty feet for some odd reason. Henry wondered if at one time the area had been set up with offices, each one having their own entrance, then later when the building had been transformed into a factory, the designers had simply left the doors where they were.

Henry waited a full thirty seconds, and when no one popped up to take a shot at him and nothing stirred, he stepped back and waved the others inside.

They entered one at a time, and once in, they split up after Henry picked teams of three.

Mary, Lyle and Cindy would search for the captured townspeople. Henry, Raven and Jimmy would see about taking the place out once and for all. If the factory was blown up somehow, then the raiders' base of power would be gone forever.

The timeline was ten minutes. They were to meet back where they started and leave with or without the townspeople.

There were doorways without doors on the opposite side of the open space and Henry pointed to them. These had to lead deeper into the factory and their intended targets. With hand signs, Henry directed each team, and like shadows wreathed in darkness, the two teams headed out, weapons drawn, safeties off, and nerves hardened for what was to come.

Chapter 25

Henry Jimmy and Raven picked a dark hallway to the right, while the other team went left. As they moved into the factory and away from the outer wall, the sounds of chaos coming from outside diminished.

Henry was on point, with Raven in the middle and Jimmy at the rear. So far there was nothing to see but abandoned offices and utility closets.

But then, Henry slowed as the hallway dog-eared to the left and he could hear the sounds of talking. He turned to Raven and Jimmy, motioning with his left hand what he was hearing, and they both nodded in understanding.

Henry was about to peer around the corner and see what was up when he suddenly heard running footsteps. He was about to warn Jimmy and Raven when five men came charging around the corner, their assault rifles in their hands and their eyes open in surprise to see three armed intruders standing in the hallway.

"What the fuck?" one of the raiders yelled as he leveled his assault rifle and prepared to shoot.

But Henry was faster, and as the first raider's finger applied pressure to the trigger of his weapon, Henry was already firing his Glock. The round caught the raider in the upper shoulder, spinning him backwards and into two other men.

Then there was chaos in the small hallway as bullets began to fly and everyone dove for cover.

Jimmy and Henry darted into one of the offices on their right, while Raven ducked behind a stainless steel water fountain in the hallway. Without a gun, all she could do was curl up tightly and ride out the storm of lead.

The five raiders began laying down covering fire and each time Henry or Jimmy tried to return fire, they were forced back inside the office.

"This isn't gonna work" Henry yelled over the gunfire. "One or two of them can keep us pinned down while the rest circle to get a better angle. We'll be shot down like dogs if we don't do something!" A piece of the wall flew off as a bullet ricocheted off the doorframe. "Shit!" Henry yelled as pieces of plaster hit his face.

"I'm all open for ideas," Jimmy replied and let loose a barrage from the shotgun. No sooner did he fire than he had to duck back or risk losing his head.

Henry's mind went into overdrive as he thought of a way to get them out of this tense situation. All the while, the raiders were stepping up their assault and Henry knew he and Jimmy had only seconds to muster a counter attack.

His arm brushed one of the grenades he was carrying, thanks to the small web belt that had been in the backpacks with the extra ammunition. Deciding he had little choice, he pulled one from the belt and prepared to throw it at the raiders.

"Wait, Henry, you can't do that!" Jimmy yelled. "Raven is out there. If you set that off, the shrapnel will get her, too!"

"I don't have a choice, Jimmy, we're all dead if I don't do something!"

And then it was too late as the raiders sent suppressing fire and Henry and Jimmy had to jump back. The raiders kept it up and Henry and Jimmy had to retreat to the back of the office. Once there, they tipped a metal desk on its side and ducked behind it.

The raiders came at them, only the small doorway slowing them down.

As bullets pinged off the desk, the two warriors could do nothing but stay low. Henry was about to throw a grenade and take his chances that the desk would save him and Jimmy from serious harm when the gunfire began to falter. Muffled yells and cries of fear filled the office and then one at a time, bodies began to strike the floor, the muffled thumps hard to ignore.

Not knowing what was going on, Henry and Jimmy stayed down. They remained like that for a full minute, and when nothing stirred, Henry slowly raised his head up over the edge of the desk.

His eyes went wide when he saw the bodies of the raiders strewn across the office floor. Standing in the center of the bodies, covered in fresh blood and still breathing heavily, stood Raven, her dark tresses hanging over her shoulders, her face covered in blood splatter.

"Jimmy, it's okay, they're dead," Henry said as he patted Jimmy's head like he was a playful puppy, while the man crouched beside him.

"What? How?" Jimmy asked.

"Have a look for yourself," Henry said as he stepped around the desk.

Raven turned to look at Henry and he saw her eyes were still wild, an animalistic fury swirling within her dark orbs like a thunderstorm. And then, as he watched, her eyes cleared and she calmed down, letting out a heavy breath of air, as if she was purging herself of her inner demon, the one that allowed her to kill like a wolf. Jimmy stepped out from behind the desk and looked down at the raiders' corpses. Each one had his throat slashed from ear to ear, the blood still seeping out of the jagged wounds. When he looked at Raven, he glanced down to her hands by her side. When he noticed the small droplets of blood dripping from her razor-sharp fingernails, it wasn't hard to figure out what had happened.

He wondered what it must have been like for the raiders to suddenly find out they had a she-demon in their midst, slashing and cutting, always moving too fast to shoot.

"Great job, Raven," Henry said, not asking any further questions. There was no need. Raven was like a mythical beast and her fighting skills were unbelievable. One day he hoped to find out exactly how she was so skilled in killing. "Okay, there's no time to lose, let's keep moving."

Raven nodded and stepped out into the hallway, while Jimmy gathered an assault rifle for each of them as well as spare ammunition. With the raiders' blood cooling on the office floor, the three warriors headed deeper into the factory.

Chapter 26

Lyle, Cindy and Mary made their way from hallway to hallway until they slowed at a junction. From this one spot, they could hear the sound of gunfire coming from outside as the raiders attempted to deal with the zombie horde. But there was something else underneath the gunfire; the sounds of cries for help.

"You hear that?" Cindy asked Mary, who nodded that she did.

"It's coming from this way," Mary said and turned to the right. Lyle was right behind her, Cindy taking up the rear. Now that adrenalin suffused her system, she barely felt her ankle, the pain just a minor nuisance.

They crept down the small hallway and slowed when it opened up into a large room with a tall ceiling and high walls.

Peering out past the doorless frame, all three of them saw the steel cages at the opposite end.

"Looks like we found them," Mary said with a smile to Lyle.

"I just pray Sharon's still alive," Lyle said.

She touched his arm, the two sharing a brief moment. "I'm sure your sister's fine, Lyle," Mary said.

Cindy broke their moment when she said, "I see three men watching the cages. We can take them easily."

Mary searched the area near the cages and spotted the three raiders. They were sitting at a small table, playing cards. She would have thought they would have been on a higher alert with the zombies outside, but then she figured to these men, their job was to watch the prisoners, and what happened outside wasn't their problem.

Mary studied the steel cages some more, trying to figure out why they were there. Then she remembered she was in a car factory. The cages had to have been for expensive tools or car parts, something that needed to be locked up. The cages were perfect prison cells for the captured townspeople.

"Okay, Mary, I'll go left and you and Lyle go right. We can take out those bastards before they know whats happening," Cindy said as she raised her M16.

"Okay, sounds good," Mary said. "You ready, Lyle?"

"Bring it on, whatever it takes to save my sister," he replied as he raised his assault rifle.

"All right, on three," Cindy said and began counting.

On 'three,' they darted out of the hallway and into the large space. They made it halfway across before the raiders realized there was someone near them they would consider a threat. As the first raider dropped his playing cards and picked up his assault rifle lying on the table, Cindy and Mary began to fire and Lyle cut loose with the rifle on full auto.

The raider who tried to pick up his weapon was the only one who knew why he died. The other two men went into the great beyond ignorant of their killers.

Bullets from Lyle's assault rifle stitched the man facing him from chest to neck, finishing him off by sending three well-placed rounds into his head. The man's head vaporized in a glorious spray of blood and bone matter, hitting the other two men in the faces. But they were beyond caring as round after round peppered their backs, blowing out their chests and spraying blood onto the headless corpse of their buddy.

Along with a clatter of guns that were never fired, the three men dropped to the floor, arms and legs twitching as nerve endings ceased to function.

Mary, Cindy and Lyle were already on the move as they raced to the cages to set the townspeople free. A few people recognized Lyle and they called out to him, begging for him to release them.

Mary was the first to the cages and she saw a heavy padlock was on each door.

"If we try to shoot these off, a ricochet could hit one of the people, we need the key."

"I'm on it," Cindy said and rushed over to the three dead raiders. Without so much as a wince at the blood and gore, she began searching their pockets for the keys. She had seen enough death over the past two years that a few fresh corpses was nothing to take notice of.

"Sharon, has anyone seen Sharon?" Lyle called out to the people inside the cages.

No one had seen her since being captured, but a few men and women said she could be in one of the other cages. Lyle asked them for what reason they were being kept and a woman said all the females were used for sex and the men for slave labor.

"Lyle, we'll find her, one thing at a time," Mary said. "Cindy, any luck?" she called out.

Cindy was still hunched over the bodies, and then she went upright and waved a set of bloody keys in her hand. "Got them!" She stood up and hobbled over to Mary, walking fine, but still favoring her bad foot.

Taking the keys from Cindy, Mary looked at them, barely noticing the blood splatter. There were only ten keys, but they all looked the same. With the people inside the cages pleading to be set free, she concentrated on finding the correct one.

She was so concerned with finding the correct keys that she never saw the three raiders that charged into the large room from the opposite side and made their way towards her and the others. Their faces were filthy, their eyes cold, only murder on their minds.

With her back to the approaching raiders, and Cindy and Lyle talking to the townspeople and trying to calm them, Mary had no idea that death was only seconds away as the first raider raised his assault rifle and prepared to shoot her in the back.

Chapter 27

Henry, Jimmy and Raven paused at a junction where three hallways joined into one large area. On the walls were bulletin boards talking about employee rights and other information a factory employee would want to know, as well as framed pictures of cars the factory once made.

Henry pointed to an overhead light and Jimmy nodded to see that it was on. "There's power in some of this building. That can only mean a generator," Henry said. "If we can find it, there should be fuel to run it," Henry said.

"It would make a hell of a bomb," Jimmy suggested.

Henry grinned, showing his teeth. "Exactly, now we're on the same wavelength, Jimmy."

"So which way?" Jimmy asked.

It was Raven who took a step forward and pointed down the west hallway. "This way, I can hear a purring sound." She pressed her left hand to the floor. "And I can feel the vibration, too."

"That's got to be the generator. Great job, Raven. Okay, let's move out. And watch yourselves, it's too damn quiet in here for my liking."

"You mean you'd prefer it if we were being shot at?" Jimmy asked.

"Yeah, maybe, at least then I'd know where the enemy is."

They began to follow the sound of the generator as they went deeper into the factory until all three of them could hear it easily. There was a set of stairs leading downward off to the left and Henry took them first, his new assault rifle leading the way.

But as soon as he stepped through the doorway, he was jumped from behind by a raider. Knocked off balance, the two men rolled down the stairs, only stopping when they reached the landing, Henry's assault rifle clattering down the steps in front of them.

Kicking free of the man, Henry came to his feet and punched the raider in the jaw, sending him reeling backwards to fall down the stairs again. As the man tumbled down into another open area, Henry was right behind him. He would have shot the raider and ended the fight quickly, but he needed information from the man.

Landing next to him, Henry bent down and was going to pick him up when the raider—who was playing possum—kicked out with his foot and knocked Henry over. The warrior fell onto the raider and they rolled around on the floor, each man trying to gain the upper hand.

Jimmy and Raven followed them down the stairs, and Jimmy had his newly acquired assault rifle aimed at the raider's head, but each time he was about to shoot, Henry would get in the way.

As for Henry, he realized this wasn't going the way he planned and he decided he needed to finish this quick. As he reached down for his Glock, the raider tackled him, sending them both to the floor once more, the Glock sliding across the floor to stop at the bottom step. Henry let out a cry of pain as the raider punched him in the kidneys, so Henry replied with a knee to the man's groin.

They continued to roll about, neither man getting the upper hand until Henry suddenly broke free and sprinted back to the stairs, as if he was a coward and running away.

The raider fell onto his back and came up with a pistol in his hand about ten feet from where Henry stood. He aimed the pistol at Henry and was about to squeeze the trigger, when he noticed two things at the same time. The first was that Henry was wearing a rather large grin on his face, as if he knew something the raider didn't. The second thing the man saw was the pin in Henry's right hand—a pin taken from one of the two grenades on the raider's web belt.

Looking down, the man realized what Henry had done and his mouth fell open and his eyes went wide with shock and fear. Knowing his time was up, Henry jumped back to the stairs while yelling at Raven and Jimmy to seek cover.

As Henry lunged up the stairs and onto the landing for protection from the blast, he caught a brief glimpse of the luckless man just as the grenade exploded, followed almost immediately by the second detonation of the other grenade.

The raider seemed to explode from within himself, his arms and legs going off in all directions as his head separated from his neck and went straight up. His torso was disintegrated into a pink mist that splattered the walls in all directions.

The entire section of the factory they were in shook on its foundation and a part of the ceiling collapsed from the detonation, and as smoke and dust filled the air, Henry crawled back to his feet.

Jimmy sat up, wiping dust from his hair and yelled, "What the fuck just happened?"

Henry shrugged. "Don't know, he must have eaten something that didn't agree with him. Come on, time's almost up, let's keep going this way. If there was a man on guard then it means we're going the right way." He retrieved his fallen assault rifle and Glock. After checking to make sure that neither gun was damaged in the blast, he led the way around the three foot, smoking crater in the cement floor, all of them careful not to step in any of the multitude of bloody body parts now strewn about like Christmas tinsel and confetti.

There was another metal door, now hanging on its hinges at the far end of the room, and one at a time they entered it, Henry once more leading the way.

Chapter 28

A split second before the raider shot Mary in the back, Lyle heard the three men's footsteps and turned to see the first man and the other raiders charging at them.

Taking in the situation in a fraction of a second, he acted without thinking, only wanting to save Mary from being shot.

As the raider began to shoot, Lyle dashed for Mary, reaching her a microsecond before the first round would have hit her. Lyle's body became a shield as he absorbed bullet after bullet, his upper torso becoming riddled with bullet holes. Lucky for Mary, but unlucky for Lyle, the raider was using expanding bullets. As soon as they entered his body, they expanded and shredded his organs. So while they practically vaporized Lyle's insides, the bullets didn't punch through him and then into Mary.

At the first gunshot, Cindy turned to face the threat and in one smooth motion, began firing her M16 on semi-automatic. The first bullets hit the raider that had tried to kill Mary, blowing his head off as well as his right arm. Then she shifted her stance and took out the other two men before they could get off even one shot. With their intestines spilling out in a bloody mess, the men collapsed to the floor, gut shot.

Seeing the men were down, Cindy maintained contact and hobbled toward them. When she reached them, the two raiders were rolling around in pain. Both looked up at her and saw her aim the M16 at them. Both men raised their hands in surrender, pleading for their lives, but Cindy was deaf to it. One at a time, she shot each man in the heart, then turned and moved as fast as her bad ankle would allow, to catch up to Mary and Lyle.

But she didn't get far. When she was halfway back, she heard a yell from behind her. Spinning, she saw four more raiders enter the large room. Shooting from the hip, the raiders darted back into the hallway from whence they came. Keeping a suppressing fire on them each time they poked their heads out, Cindy held them at bay.

"Mary, we've got more company, we need to get going!" she yelled. She flicked the selector on the rifle from semi-automatic to single shot and then fired three more times before popping the magazine out and sliding in a new one. Fully loaded, she sent one round at the doorway and then hunkered down to wait for the raiders' next move.

Behind her, Mary was sitting on the floor. Lyle was lying on his shredded back, his head on her lap. Blood spilled from the corner of his mouth, and each time he coughed, bloody bubbles shot out. There was no question he was dying, as his insides were practically soup.

In the steel cage behind Mary, a few stray rounds had hit the townspeople and the wounded lay on the floor as others attended to them. Wails of sadness filled the air but Mary heard none of it. Her whole world at the moment was Lyle as he lay dying.

Lyle coughed when he tried to speak, then he managed to utter a few words. At first, Mary couldn't understand him but then the words made sense.

"Promise me you'll save Sharon," he whispered through blood-coated lips.

"Of course I will, Lyle. Don't you worry; we'll find her and bring her home." She brushed his sweat-soaked hair off his brow as tears ran down her cheeks. "Oh God, Lyle, I'm so sorry."

"Don't be. I guess it's my time. Did...did you get hit?"

She shook her head, her hair falling over her shoulders to hang down on each side of her face. "No, I'm fine...thanks to you."

"I'm glad you're gonna be fine." He coughed some more, his entire body spasming as he tried to suck in one more breath.

"Mary, tell me something, even though it doesn't matter anymore."

"Anything," she cried.

"Could you...could you have loved me?"

"Yes, Lyle, easily. So easily you wouldn't believe," she cried, the tears now coming in droves. They dripped from her chin to land on his chest.

"That's good...'cause believe it or not...I already loved y..." He never finished his sentence, his head slumping to the side, his chest rising and falling for the last time as his eyes closed in final sleep.

Mary's shoulders shook with grief as she held Lyle, cradling his head against her chest. She rocked back and forth, crying not only for him, but for herself. She could have taken the chance he had offered and she could have found happiness with him. Now that it was too late, she knew it had been possible. But now it was all gone, like smoke in the wind, lost on the first breeze.

At first Mary didn't hear Cindy yelling at her, but slowly, as the seconds passed and she set Lyle's head down on the blood-soaked floor, the sounds of her surroundings penetrated her grief-stricken haze. She heard people yelling behind her, gunshots, and Cindy calling her name.

"Mary, come on, dammit, snap out of it! I can't hold these bastards off forever. Get those cages open so we can get the hell out of here!"

Wiping her eyes, Mary straightened her shoulders and nodded to herself. Lyle had sacrificed himself so she could live. So his sister could live. She wouldn't throw that chance away for either of them. Standing, she picked up the keys and moved back to the first cage. By luck alone, it was the second key she tried that was the correct one. Unlocking the padlock, she took it off the door and tossed it away, then pulled the cage door open.

"You're free!" she yelled. "Go stand by Cindy and wait for me to get the other cages open. Then we're getting out of here!"

The townspeople exited the cage as fast as humanly possible, others carrying the wounded. Cindy waved them over and pointed to the fallen raiders and their guns. As she kept the other raiders at bay, a few of the men ran to the fallen weapons. Once they scooped them up, Cindy had help.

With four people now laying down covering fire, the raiders had no choice but to retreat until they had greater numbers.

Meanwhile, Mary had unlocked the other cages, and one by one, everyone exited them until all were out and ready to leave.

With Mary in the lead, she looked over her shoulder at Lyle's body one last time, then she turned forward, and with Cindy by her side, the two female warriors began to lead the townspeople to freedom.

"I hope the others are doing as good as we are, 'cause times about up," Cindy yelled to Mary as they made their way out of the large room and into a hallway.

Mary didn't answer. Lyle was dead.

If that was how the others were doing, then she didn't wish the same success on any of them.

Chapter 29

With Henry in the lead, they entered through the damaged door. A round hit the wall so close to Henry's face that he felt the air move. As he ducked back, he caught a glance at the room and what was in it.

It was a large room and the backup generator, one of three scattered throughout the factory, was in the right hand corner. It was guarded by four raiders, each with a weapon aimed at the doorway.

"Get back, it's not safe," Henry snapped as Jimmy tried to shoot at the raiders, the four men hiding behind a stack of wooden crates. "Wait, Jimmy, don't shoot!"

Jimmy halted at the last second, his finger a fraction of an ounce away from pulling the trigger.

"What's wrong? Why the hell not?" Jimmy snapped back. "They're trapped in there. Let's take 'em out and finish this shit."

"We can't, at least not yet," Henry said. "Didn't you see what was behind the men?"

"No," Jimmy said and poked his head around the doorframe. As soon as he did, bullets ricocheted off the frame and zipped through the door. He pulled his head back as the frame was splintered by bullets. "I saw steel drums, fifty gallon by the look of 'em"

Henry nodded. "Yeah, probably. And do you know what's in them?"

Jimmy didn't and his eyebrows went up as if to tell Henry that, *no he didn't and to just spit it out.*

"The fuel for the generator has to be in them. The raiders must have brought it all down here to keep it safe instead of storing it outside like in the old days," Henry explained. "That's why there's four men guarding it. It's their fuel reserves."

"So that's just great. If we can't shoot at them and they can at us, then how the hell are we supposed to get in there?"

Henry grinned. "I have an idea."

"So spill it," Jimmy prompted.

Raven tapped Henry on the shoulder and pointed to the way they'd come. "I'm gonna go check to make sure no one's coming," she told him.

He nodded and she moved away, careful not to step in any of the body parts on the floor.

"Well?" Jimmy asked again.

Henry replied by pulling a grenade from his web belt and holding it up for Jimmy to see.

"No fucking way," Jimmy said. "But what about us? There's no way we can get away in time. And we don't know if the girls are safe yet? You can't just blow it up."

Henry's reply was to turn back to the doorway and poke his head around. After a flurry of shots peppered the doorframe like he expected, he tossed the grenade into the room.

It landed two yards from the four men, then bounced and rolled until it came up near them, to the left side of the stack of crates. One of the raiders looked down, saw the grenade a few feet away, and yelled as loud as he could in warning.

"Grenade!"

All four men popped up and ran in all directions to escape the impending blast, Henry and Jimmy forgotten for the moment.

Jimmy, knowing his death was imminent, fell to the floor and covered his head with his hands, squeezing his eyes shut to await the fiery explosion that would probably take out the entire section of the factory they were in.

He expected Henry to also be cowering as he waited for the inevitable blast, but instead of falling down and covering himself, he strode into the generator room like he had nothing to fear, his assault rifle leading the way.

The four men were still running away from the grenade, not having covered more than a few feet of distance, and Henry began firing precise shots at each man. His aim was perfect; only when he knew he had a shot did he take one and he only aimed for body shots to decrease the chance of a miss.

In seconds, all four raiders were down and dead, Henry standing over them, checking to make sure each one was truly dead.

Jimmy peeked through his closed eyelids and then stood up, realizing the explosion he expected wasn't coming. Rising to his feet, he entered the generator room to see Henry standing amongst the dead raiders. "But, I don't get it," he said as he looked around.

Henry walked over to the grenade and picked it up. "I didn't pull the pin, Jimmy," he said as he went to the generator to see how he could jury rig it into a bomb.

"Oh, you didn't pull the pin…nice." He walked closer to Henry, his face now angry. "Well you could have fucking told me that, couldn't you?"

"Nah, watching you squirm like that was priceless. I swear to God, if you could have kissed your own ass goodbye, you would have," Henry chuckled.

"Ha, ha, old man, very fucking funny. Don't quit your day job."

Raven appeared at the doorway and Jimmy and Henry spun with guns aimed at her. She raised her hands and smiled as she entered the room.

"Don't shoot, it's me, I surrender."

"What's the status?" Henry asked her, returning to study the generator.

"It's clear," she said. "I saw a few raiders but they ran past me. I heard one of them talking and it sounds pretty bad outside. The deaders are winning."

Henry nodded. "Good, that's how we want it." He waved her to him. "Come here, I need something from you," he said.

She padded over, and when she was close enough, he reached out and pulled a few strands of black hair from her head.

"Ouch, what the hell?"

"Sorry, honey, but it's for the greater good." He grabbed Jimmy's arm and pulled him close as he handed him the grenade. "Here, hold this for a second. I need a second pair of hands to get this done."

Not understanding, Jimmy did what he was told, and as he and Raven watched Henry, the older warrior began making a bomb with a timer.

A few minutes later had the three friends running out of the generator room, up the stairs and back to the rendezvous with the others.

Back in the generator room, on the machine itself, was a contraption of Henry's own invention.

It was simple in its design, but at the same time wasn't an exact science.

On the generator, surrounded by open steel drums of gasoline, sat the grenade Henry had thrown into the room.

The pin was now pulled and the hair he took from Raven was wrapped around the handle, preventing it from opening and thus going off.

There was a lit cigarette also attached to the grenade by a strand of hair and it slowly burned down, a makeshift fuse for the man with no time for anything fancier.

The pack of smokes was on the floor, the dead raider it was taken from not needing it.

As the cigarette burned down, sooner rather than later it would reach the hair, and once that happened, the hair would burn and the handle would pop open.

Three seconds later, the generator room would be nothing but an inferno of exploding fuel; barrels and barrels of it, a powder keg only minutes from erupting.

Chapter 30

Halfway to the large main room where they would all meet, Henry, Jimmy and Raven became pinned down by a raider. The man was using a high caliber rifle, and every time he shot at them, the round would punch through whatever the three friends were hiding behind.

Jimmy let out a squeak when a bullet flew through the file cabinet he was hiding behind, leaving a finger-sized hole an inch from his face.

"Jesus Christ that was close!" he yelled to Henry and Raven who were hiding a few feet away. "Get this fucking guy, Henry! That shit downstairs is gonna blow any second!"

Henry knew Jimmy was right. At any moment, the bomb would go off, taking out this entire section of the factory.

They were in another large room set up for cubicles. Overhead, were large air conditioning units and circular ductwork. The entire area had the feel of once being used for something more industrial, and was later changed to be used for office space.

The raider was hiding behind a desk, the most convenient protection in the cubicles, and he sent bullet after bullet at the companions as he slowly zeroed in on his targets.

Sneaking a peek around the copy machine he was behind, Henry had to duck back quickly when a shot took off half the machine in a spray of plastic and glass.

But he saw what he wanted, a chink in the raider's defense. Unfortunately, he was at the wrong angle to take advantage of it.

But Raven wasn't.

He called out to her to get her attention, and with hand signals, told her what he wanted her to do. She nodded and proceeded to crawl to the left, circling around to take her shot.

Peering around a stack of boxes filled with paper printouts, she leveled her rifle and took her shot.

The desk was a standard one and the raider didn't realize that though his upper body was protected from being shot thanks to the desk, his feet up to his ankles weren't.

As Raven stretched out on her stomach, she had a perfect line of sight to the raider's left ankle.

Sighting carefully, she let loose on full auto, blowing the man's leg off at the shin and causing him to yell out in pain.

He dropped to the floor and screamed as blood gushed from his missing foot.

Henry jumped up, ready to sprint and take the man out for good when he saw from his vantage point that the man wasn't down for the count. As the raider screamed in agony, he took a grenade from his web belt, ready to pull the pin and toss it at Raven. He had decided if he was going to die, then he was going to take his killer with him.

Henry saw he had half a second to figure out how to stop the man cold or Raven would be nothing but bloody bits.

His eyes searched left and right to no avail, and then he looked up. On the ceiling, directly over the raider, was an air conditioning unit.

It was large, four feet wide by four feet, with a metal exterior.

Not knowing if it would work but out of options, Henry aimed at the metal supports holding the unit to the ceiling. Bullets sent sparks in all directions as the rounds shredded the supports and carved divots in the ceiling.

With a loud ripping of metal, the last support, unable to support the unit on its own, snapped free, the unit falling to the floor to land flat on the raider, just as the man pulled the pin on the grenade, and had his arm pulled back over his head to throw it.

"Get down!" Henry yelled, but it wasn't necessary. Just as the man was flattened into a meat pancake, the grenade went off.

The metal casing of the unit bulged outward and the unit jumped six inches into the air before falling back to the floor, but the weight of the condenser and motor was enough to contain all of the blast and force it down into the floor.

As smoke curled up around the unit and their ears rang from the muffled sound of the grenade, Henry peered over the desk the raider was hiding behind to see a slurry of red seeping out from under the ruined a/c unit.

"Okay, let's move out. Double time it, this guy cost us time we don't have."

Jimmy and Raven jumped to their feet and they took off at a run. Only two minutes had passed, but with time so precious, each second gone was one more they didn't have to waste.

Chapter 31

"Where the hell are they?" Cindy asked Mary as they waited in the large room that had the multitude of doors leading to the outside.

All around them, the rescued townspeople waited. A few wanted to leave now but Cindy had explained what was going on outside and that the best way for everyone to reach Cement City alive was to stick together. Of course, a few didn't listen and had left.

Whether they had made it past the zombie gauntlet was unknown.

Mary checked her wristwatch to see it was a few minutes over the time Henry, Raven and Jimmy should have returned. Biting her lip, she looked at the townspeople, studying their faces. It was as she scanned the crowd that she spotted a beautiful woman in the back talking to some others. The resemblance to Lyle was uncanny. Mary stared at her for more than a minute and then stood up and walked over to her.

"Excuse me," Mary said. "I was wondering if by chance your name is Sharon."

"Yes it is, why?"

"Was Lyle your brother?"

"What do you mean 'was'?"

"You mean you don't know?"

"Know what? What are you talking about?" Sharon looked nervous, seeing the sadness in Mary's eyes.

Mary quickly filled Sharon in on what happened to Lyle. When she was through, Sharon was in shock.

"You mean that man who was shot at the cages was Lyle? That was my brother?" She began to cry. "I...I didn't know. Everyone was pushing and yelling and I was forced out of the cage, and then I had to help a friend who got shot. Oh no, oh God, no," she cried as tears ran down her cheeks.

"He was a good man and his last wish was that I make sure you get home safely," Mary said sadly, the tears threatening to come again. Only with a force of will did she keep them down.

Her conversation was cut short when gunshots sounded from one of the hallways leading out of the main room. Cindy and all the townspeople that were armed with guns taken from dead raiders, all aimed them at the opening and waited for whoever appeared. Fingers were tense on triggers and sweat dripped from foreheads, the tension heavy.

And then Henry appeared as he ran into the room, Jimmy and Raven right behind him. Raven sprayed her assault rifle into the hallway and the distinct sounds of screams filled the large room.

"Don't shoot, they're with us!" Cindy yelled at the townspeople as she jumped in front of them, making sure someone didn't accidentally think Henry and company were raiders.

Luckily, no one fired and guns were lowered as Henry, Jimmy and Raven were welcomed with open arms. But Henry didn't stop running as he joined Cindy and Mary who came up beside him.

"There's no time for talking," he said quickly. "We've got seconds at most before this whole place goes up. Go, get going! Now!"

"But where do we go?" Mary asked.

"The parking lot. We have to try for that transit bus. It's the only way to get everyone back to the town safely." No sooner did he finish speaking then the entire building shook as if an earthquake had begun. There was a muffled boom, followed by a louder one, and soon the windows were shattering in their frames and anything not secured in some way was falling over.

"Jesus Christ!" Jimmy yelled as he struggled to stay on his feet.

"Go, get outside! Get moving!" Henry yelled and he sprayed bullets from his assault rifle into the ceiling. That got everyone moving, and using all the doors, they began to file out.

Mary stayed behind with Henry as he made sure there were no stragglers.

A few raiders popped up at the hallway Henry had used and he shot at them, making them duck back.

"Come on, this whole place is about to fall in! I bet there was trapped natural gas in the lines and now that's catching, too!" Another vibration shook the building and machines tumbled over to crash across the floor.

More raiders appeared and Henry spun, shooting two in the chest, and sending them to the floor in a bloody spray of gore. But he hadn't seen the other man that had managed to get to cover before Henry shot the man's two buddies.

Henry, thinking he had taken down the threat, turned and began shoving people out of the factory.

"Mary, go, I'm right behind you!" Henry yelled to her as he shoved her in the back

"But what about you?" she yelled.

"I'm coming, I just want to make sure everyone gets out in one piece, now stop arguing and go!"

A section of the ceiling fell in, sending up a loose cloud of dust and flying cement, and Mary nodded and did as she was told. Henry watched her leave and then went back to help a man carry another man who was wounded.

Once they were through the door, he went back for any more stragglers. With the structure coming down around him, he had to save as many people as he could.

He was about to leave, seeing that it looked like everyone was gone, when the raider who had snuck into the room came up behind Henry and fired his gun.

Only the gun didn't shoot.

The raider hadn't kept track of his bullets and his magazine was spent.

Henry, hearing the click over the roar of the collapsing building, spun around and prepared to shoot the raider with his assault rifle, but the man acted fast and he lunged at Henry, wrapping his arms around the deadlands warrior as both men fell to the floor.

Henry struggled to fight back but the raider had him in a bear hug and had trapped his arms between them. The butt of the assault rifle dug into Henry's stomach and made him growl with pain.

The raider laughed as he kneed Henry in the groin, causing the warrior to see stars. With his arms trapped and his legs useless, Henry used the only thing he had at his disposal—his teeth.

As the raider lay on top of him, laughing at his helplessness, his knee in Henry's groin, Henry leaned forward and locked his teeth on the raider's nose. Clamping down tightly, he began to wiggle his head as blood shot into his mouth and the nose began to separate from the raider's face.

Letting loose a painful roar, the raider yanked his head back, and Henry spit out the quarter inch tip of cartilage, grinning fiendishly, his teeth and lips coated in the man's blood.

"Why you dirty fucker," the raider hissed and punched Henry in the face, causing the warrior to see stars.

Henry felt no guilt about what he'd done. There was no honor in a battle to the death, only one man living and the other man dying. He planned on being the former and how he got to that point was irrelevant.

Another blow struck Henry's jaw and he lost consciousness for a second before coming back to reality a moment later.

Desperate, he tried using his forehead to crack it onto what was left of the raider's nose, but the man snapped his head back, onto the move and not willing to get suckered twice.

Henry was fast realizing he was overmatched. The raider had more than fifty pounds on Henry and it was all muscle, and he was at least a half foot taller.

After receiving another blow to the face, Henry spit blood—his own this time—and struggled to free his arms.

Then he was being pulled to his feet as the raider picked him up and held him off the floor. Before Henry could try and kick the man, he was being carried across the room like he was no more than a child, his back coming up hard against the cinder-block wall. His breath left him in a whoosh from the impact and he saw stars yet again. All around the two brawling men, the factory was collapsing in a spray of dust, steel and cement.

Henry kicked out with his knee and managed to connect with the raider but the man acted as if nothing had happened. With his nose spewing blood over his lips and down his chin, he looked like some maniacal murderer from a bad horror movie.

The man punched Henry in the kidney, causing him to see flashes of light, brighter than before, and while Henry tried to recover, to suck in a breath of air, he suddenly found the raider's ham-sized hands wrapped around his throat.

"Now you die, fucker," the raider hissed.

Henry couldn't breathe, his heartbeat pounding in his head, and though he punched the raider repeatedly in the chest and side, the man refused to let him go.

As darkness began to descend and Henry slid into oblivion, he knew this was one battle he'd lost.

Chapter 32

A split second before Henry blacked out, he heard a muffled gunshot and felt warm spray hit his face.

No sooner did this happen then the death grip on his neck loosened. He felt himself fall to the floor and his legs came up under him. Gasping and wheezing, he opened his eyes to see Mary standing over him, her eyes wide with fear and worry. In her hand was her .38, the barrel still smoking, a thin wisp trailing off into the dusty air.

Henry looked down to see the raider that had been on the verge of killing him was now prone on the floor, his head lying in Henry's lap.

Or what was left of his head.

The right side of the raider's face was all but missing, only jagged skull sticking out of the massive hole, brains dripping out like cold motor oil. The left side of the raider's head was intact but there was a burn mark, black, around his ear. This was where Mary had placed the muzzle of her gun before shooting the man in the head.

Henry pushed the corpse off him, and with a hacking and coughing fit, went to his knees. Mary helped him stand, and though dizzy, he forced himself to snap out of it, knowing there was no time to lose.

"Out...side, now," he gasped and Mary helped him walk. "My gun," he wheezed.

She paused when she saw his assault rifle and she left him to pick it up. Still dizzy, he almost dropped to the floor when he was alone, but she joined him again and caught him before he could fall.

"Let's go," he said softly. Like he was a geriatric and she the dutiful daughter, Mary helped Henry out of the factory.

No sooner did they exit the building then the ceiling fell in, crushing the raider's body as well as the other dead men shot down by Henry.

When they were out of the building, Henry immediately began to feel better, sucking in the relatively clean air. There was the taste of smoke in the air but compared to the dust and grit filling the inside of the factory, the air was crisp and clean, the cloudless sky allowing moon and starlight to bathe the area.

"How are you doing?" she asked as she led him away from the factory. With each step he took he felt better, and by the time they were twenty feet away, he was feeling well enough to walk on his own.

"Better, much better, actually. Thanks, Mary, you saved my ass back there," he said while rubbing his sore throat. There were red marks on his neck from the raider's large hands.

She grinned slightly. "I'm just glad I decided to come back when I didn't see you leave."

"Me too," he said and coughed one more time, as if he was clearing out the last of it. With him almost back to peak performance, they began walking to the end of the building where they would round it and be at the parking lot.

When they reached the corner, Raven was waiting for them. She took one look at Henry and was about to ask what was wrong with him when he held his hands up to stop her.

"It doesn't matter, give me an update," he said, his voice hoarse from being choked.

"Okay then, fine," Raven said flatly. "Everyone's in the bus and Jimmy's driving. The keys were in the ignition but the damn thing won't start. He's messing with it now."

Henry nodded. "And the townspeople?"

"Most made it to the bus but deaders are everywhere. A lot of people got taken down and killed," she said.

As if to illustrate her statement, three ghouls came from out of the shadows and lunged at them. Raven spun on her heels and took them down with a hail of bullets from her assault rifle. The bodies danced a jig until headshots put them down for good.

"Good, okay, let's get to the bus and get the hell out of here," Henry said, his voice slightly stronger. "But before we go, let me clear us a path." He pulled his last grenade from his web belt and stepped around the corner of the building.

His eyes took in the scene immediately.

There was absolute chaos in all directions, and in many ways when he imagined what Hell on Earth would be like, this image was at the top of the list.

In every direction were the walking dead, some shambling around but most were feeding on the corpses of the townspeople and the raiders they had killed.

The backdrop to this were two infernos. One was from the pickup truck Henry had used as a diversion. The flames had spread in the dry grass and most of the perimeter near the fence was burning, a choking black smoke spewing off in all directions. The second one was the factory itself. The generator room had been close to this side of the building, and when it had exploded, the entire side of the factory collapsed in on itself, the flames reaching to the heavens as smoke billowed out in thick pillars.

The zombies fought over body parts, tearing at organs and chewing intestines, their faces bloody and covered in gore. Many took an arm or a leg and staggered away to feed in private, these ghouls not into the act of sharing.

The rancid smell of burning meat suffused the air, making Henry want to gag. But he fought off the urge, knowing there was no time for weakness.

Across the parking lot was the transit bus, and Henry could see Cindy and a few townspeople standing around it, shooting at the zombies that tried to get at them.

Seeing the best place to toss the grenade, Henry pulled the pin, waited an extra second, and let it fly, the small orb spinning through the air to detonate while still airborne.

Twenty-five ghouls in the area felt the brunt of the blast, the shrapnel taking off limbs and heads as if they were made of paper mache.

As the rumble of the blast reverberated throughout the parking lot, Henry, Mary and Raven made their break for the bus, shooting as they went, taking down ghoul after ghoul in a storm of lead.

When Henry's assault rifle ran dry, he tossed it away and pulled his Glock, now taking only head shots.

One ghoul came for him with its lips spread wide in a guttural moan and he shot it right through its open mouth. The upper bridgework was blown apart, bits of teeth shooting up into the zombie's brain like shrapnel. It fell over dead, limbs twitching in the firelight.

As they made their way through the charnel house of death, each of them tried not to look at the victims. Henry stepped over a prone corpse and when he did, the eyes opened and the remaining hand reached for him. He could see the victim wasn't a zombie, only a person suffering in absolute agony. Knowing there was nothing he could do but show mercy, he shot the victim in the head, ending the suffering as best he could.

When they reached the bus, Cindy ran out of ammunition for her assault rifle and she threw it at an approaching zombie. The gun spun end over end and cracked the ghoul in the face. Then one of the townspeople shot it in the head and it was down for good.

"Everyone, get on the bus!" Henry yelled as he kicked a ghoul away and began shoving people onto the bus. The vehicle was an older model, with a carburetor and no air conditioning. If the dead hadn't walked, the bus would have been put out to pasture or sold off for being too old.

Once more he was the last one in.

"Jimmy, close the door!" he yelled as he stepped on the bus. Jimmy reached out and hit the button to close the door, then looked at Henry. He was about to ask why Henry looked like shit when Henry cut him off when he said, "Talk to me Jimmy, you got this thing running?"

"I'm trying but it won't start and I'm afraid I'm gonna kill the battery."

"Okay, then just give it a few seconds to rest. Maybe you flooded it." He willed his voice to sound calm. "Just relax, we're safe in here for the moment, they can't get in." He turned around to look at all the people behind him. The bus was filled to capacity.

Mary and Cindy were with a woman Henry didn't know and he wondered if she was Lyle's sister. Raven was in the seat to his right and she was looking out the window. She didn't like what she saw as the ghouls massed outside the vehicle.

While they waited to try the engine one more time, the dead began surrounding the bus. In less than two minutes there were more than sixty ghouls, all banging on the sides, their hands reaching up to the high windows.

Everyone was scared and felt trapped, and Henry didn't blame them.

"What is it about buses and deaders, Henry, huh? Will you tell me please?" Jimmy asked, referring to their time when they were trapped on a greyhound bus and surrounded by zombies. They almost hadn't made it out of there alive, and only luck had been with them and allowed them to live and talk about it.

"I don't know, Jimmy, I guess we're just lucky," Henry smiled wanly. He nodded to the ignition on the dashboard. "Go 'head, try again, but be gentle this time."

Jimmy did as he was told, Henry having a calming effect on him. Being ever so gentle, he turned the ignition key.

The engine began to turn over, revving and whirring and then it began to sputter.

"Okay, Jimmy, now give it a little gas. But just a little!" Henry yelled, not wanting Jimmy to floor it and flood the carburetor.

He did as he was told, pressing lightly on the gas pedal and the engine slowly began to even out until it was purring softly.

"That did it, it's running!" Jimmy yelled so everyone could hear him.

A cheer went up through the bus and clapping ensued.

Henry took the seat next to Raven, relieved to finally be resting.

"How much gas we got?" Henry asked.

"A quarter of a tank if the gauge is reading right," Jimmy replied.

"Good, that's more than enough. Okay, Jimmy, take it slow and get going. First we have to go get Sue, then we have people to reunite with family."

With more clapping and cheering, as well as a lot of hugging, Jimmy put the transmission into gear and the bus' tires began to turn.

The zombies were crushed beneath the wheels when they refused to move, and other than a few bumps as bodies were driven over and crushed into paste, the large bus easily made its way through the zombie horde.

Swinging the bus around to face the chain-link gate leading to the main road, Jimmy drove right through it, sparks lighting the night as the large vehicle crashed through the gate easily, the steel posts banging off the windshield but not damaging it.

With a surging of the engine, the bus continued down the road, leaving the factory to burn, and the zombies to stumble about as they fed on corpses of townspeople and raiders alike, tearing and chewing, their pale faces reflected in the firelight, casting long shadows on the blood-soaked ground.

Epilogue

Ben was fast asleep in his bed on the north side of Cement City when he was suddenly pulled from his slumber. He had heard a noise and it sounded like it was right in the room with him.

As his eyes popped open, his right hand reached for the handgun on the nightstand, but before he could grab it, a hand went to his mouth and a large blade pressed into the skin of his throat, right over his jugular.

As the blade touched his flesh, a thin rivulet of blood dripped from a small cut, attesting to the sharpness of the weapon. All the intruder had to do was lean on the handle slightly and the edge would slice into his neck, killing him when it severed his jugular.

Whoever had managed to get into his home now had him dead to rights.

"Now, Ben, I'm going to remove my hand from your mouth. You so much as sneeze and you're gonna have to wear turtlenecks to cover up that nasty neck wound I'm gonna give you. Nod once if you understand what I'm telling you. And do it slowly or risk getting that turtleneck anyway."

Not having a choice, Ben did as he was told. Ever so slowly, he nodded and was relieved when the pressure of the blade lessened.

A small oil lamp on his nightstand was lit, allowing the intruder and himself to see each other easily. The intruder removed his hand.

"Watson," Ben spit. "I should have known."

"Not happy to see me? That's okay, this isn't a social visit."

Ben's eyes went to the nightstand drawer but no sooner did he do this then Henry held up the black box. It had been hidden in the drawer and Henry had found it before waking Ben up.

"Looking for this?"

Ben said nothing.

"Listen up, Ben, 'cause I'm only gonna say this once. We rescued the people you sent us after. Lyle's dead, a casualty. His sister is safe, however. In the morning they'll all be arriving in a city bus we took from the raiders' base. And as for the raiders, they're history, they won't be bothering your town again."

"So that was the smoke I saw earlier?" Ben asked.

"Damn straight."

"So if you did what we sent you to do, then why are you here now?" Ben asked.

"'Cause I don't trust you to keep up your end of the bargain," Henry replied.

"So what now?"

"Simple, give me the code to disarm the box and I'll let you live. I'll leave right now and you'll never see me or my friends again. Despite everything that's happened, I can't really find fault with you. Your son died and you wanted vengeance, but you passed on it for a chance to help your fellow people. I can respect that."

"And if I don't give you the code?" Ben asked.

Henry shrugged casually, the movement causing the panga to press deeper into Ben's throat. The man gasped in fear but he did a good job of hiding it well. "Then I'll cut your throat right now and me and my friends will figure out how to take off the bracelets ourselves. But at least you'll be dead. So, what's it gonna be?"

Ben said nothing and Henry found it amusing that the man was actually giving his proposition some thought. In the end, if the man wanted to live, there was only one way this would go.

"Fine," Ben finally said and he told Henry the numbers that made up the code.

"How do I know it's the correct one?" Henry asked casually, as if the two men were having a beer on the patio.

"It's my son's birthday. I thought it would be poetic."

Henry handed Ben the black box. "Here, you punch it in. If you're lying, then we can die together. Oh and just in case you think that's fine, all my friends are in different parts of the city. I think Jimmy is at the mayor's house and Cindy is over where you store your gasoline. If she blows up, you're entire shipment of fuel and half the town goes with her."

"You're lying," Ben said coldly.

Henry leaned over the bed so his face was only inches from Ben's. The two men locked gazes.

"Then I guess you'll have to call my bluff and see what happens. Though you won't be here to find out. See, you'll be in a thousand tiny and bloody pieces; we'll both be."

Ben stared at Henry's eyes for another minute and when Henry's gaze never faltered, Ben finally turned away.

Carefully so as not to press the panga into his throat, Ben punched in the numbers. Whether they were the same ones he had given Henry, the deadlands warrior didn't know, but a second after Ben finished, Henry saw the red light on his bracelet go out. He hid the feeling of relief that flooded through him and knew his friends were even now cutting their bracelets off.

"You may have seen through my plan, Watson, and I'll tell you this much, you were right. I wasn't going to live up to my end of the deal. As soon as you came back, I was going to blow you all to Hell. But know this, Watson, this isn't over. As long as I'm alive, you have an enemy. One of these days, I'll find you and when I do, Jimmy, you, and whoever you're with will be killed very slowly and very painfully. I will get my revenge for what your people did to my son."

Henry stared at Ben for a full minute, remaining silent, thinking about what he'd just heard.

Ben was about to say something when Henry spoke up first, stopping the man.

"I'm sorry you feel that way, Ben, I truly do," Henry sighed as if he was disappointed. "Believe it or not, I really was going to let you live if you gave me the code. I'm a man of my word. But I learned a long time ago not to let an enemy live. No man should have to keep looking over his shoulder, waiting for someone to stick a knife in his back."

Without preamble, before Ben realized what Henry was going to do, as Henry's voice never changed in pitch the entire time he spoke—it was calm and soft—he pushed the panga into Ben's throat, severing the man's jugular as he slid the blade from left to right, slicing more than two inches into his throat.

Blood geysered out to splatter the ceiling and Henry took a step back, away from the worst of the blood spray.

Ben let out one gasp of air and then blood spilled from his mouth, his eyelids fluttering as his hands went to his throat to stop the flow of blood.

Plasma squirted through his fingers as they slid inside the massive gash in his throat.

It took less than a minute for Ben to bleed out, the sheets becoming soaked and turning a dark red.

When Ben stopped twitching, his eyes unmoving, Henry walked over to the foot of the bed and cleaned his panga where the sheets were still pristine, then he wiped his face of blood splatter and lastly, he cut off the bracelet on his ankle, tossing it onto Ben's chest.

Spying the handgun on the nightstand, he took it, putting it into the back of his pants; he could use it in trade at the next town.

He already had the bullets for it, having taken them out of the gun before waking Ben. There was a reason why he'd left the gun out in plain view. If the man had tried for it, the look on his face when he squeezed the trigger only to find it wasn't loaded would have been priceless.

Leaving the way he had entered the room, Henry closed the door behind him, only the soft sound of blood dripping off the bed and onto the floor remaining.

"What the hell, that ain't a fair trade!" a man in a worn leather jacket yelled angrily. He was coated in dust with a face that looked a lot like road kill. Acne and blackheads covered him like a road map.

"It's a fair trade, mister, I swear, that's the best I can do. We need to make a living 'round here, too, ya know," the old woman pleaded from behind the counter of the trading post. It was located at the main gate of the small town of Birmingham, Nevada.

"Bullshit, that's bullshit and you know it. You're tryin' ta screw me, and now that I know about it you're tryin' ta deny it."

Before the old woman knew what was happening, the man drew a battered Browning from his jacket and aimed the muzzle directly at the woman's forehead. Her eyes went wide as she came to the realization she was about to die.

"So now I'm gonna take everything you got and leave you with a fucking hole in your head!" the man yelled, spittle flying from his cracked lips.

He'd been on the road for more than a month, narrowly escaping the walking dead more times than he could count.

He'd killed more men than he could count since the first contaminated rain fell, changing the world forever, and almost all of them hadn't deserved it.

He believed in this new world of the walking dead. That only the strong survived, and goddammit, he was the strongest!

A malevolent smile crossed his lips as his finger began to squeeze the trigger and blow the old woman's head clean off her shoulders. Knowing she was dead, she closed her eyes and waited to feel the lead slug impact her skull.

The woman jumped as the gunshot filled the trading post, but a split second later, she realized she was still alive. She wasn't shot!

Opening her eyes a tad, she caught the end of the life of the man threatening her.

A bullet impacted the back of the man's head, sending the upper half of his scalp and forehead into the air. As the man fell forward, the Browning fell from his grip to clatter on the counter.

The man's brains blew out and around the old woman. Miraculously, not one bit of brain matter landed on her.

The fresh corpse was slammed forward and then it rolled to the floor, the man's eyes still open, not understanding what had occurred.

The smell of cordite and blood filled the trading post as the old woman glanced past the counter to the stranger standing before her with a 9mm Glock in his hand, smoke still drifting from the muzzle.

He wasn't overly tall, a shy over five eight, but his broad shoulders and grim visage gave him the look of a man six feet plus. His muscular arms were visible, the tank top he wore also showing off his powerful chest and the few gray hairs peeking through above the line of the shirt.

As the old woman's eyes went higher, she saw a strong chin, slightly covered in stubble, and as she looked higher she saw the cold eyes of a killer. But there was something else swimming in those steely orbs, something that reminded her of mercy, of compassion.

His hair was cut short, and the once brown locks were now splattered with gray, giving him the look of a man much older than his forty plus years.

'You all right, ma'am?" the man said as he took a step closer, one eye always on the corpse just in case the man was somehow *not* dead.

"I...I'm fine, yes, many thanks. I thought I was a goner."

He grunted in reply as moved closer to the counter. Kneeling down over the corpse, he rifled through the man's leather jacket. He pulled out some spare ammo for the Browning, found a hunting knife and a few odds and ends, such as a cigarette lighter and a small box of toothpicks.

He also found a roll of cash, hundred dollar bills by the looks of it, and as he rolled the wad in his hand, he casually tossed it aside. He had toilet paper, he didn't need any more.

"Do you have a name, mister?" the old woman asked, still shaky from her brush with death.

"Sure, the name's Henry Watson."

LOOK FOR DEAD ARMY IN 2011

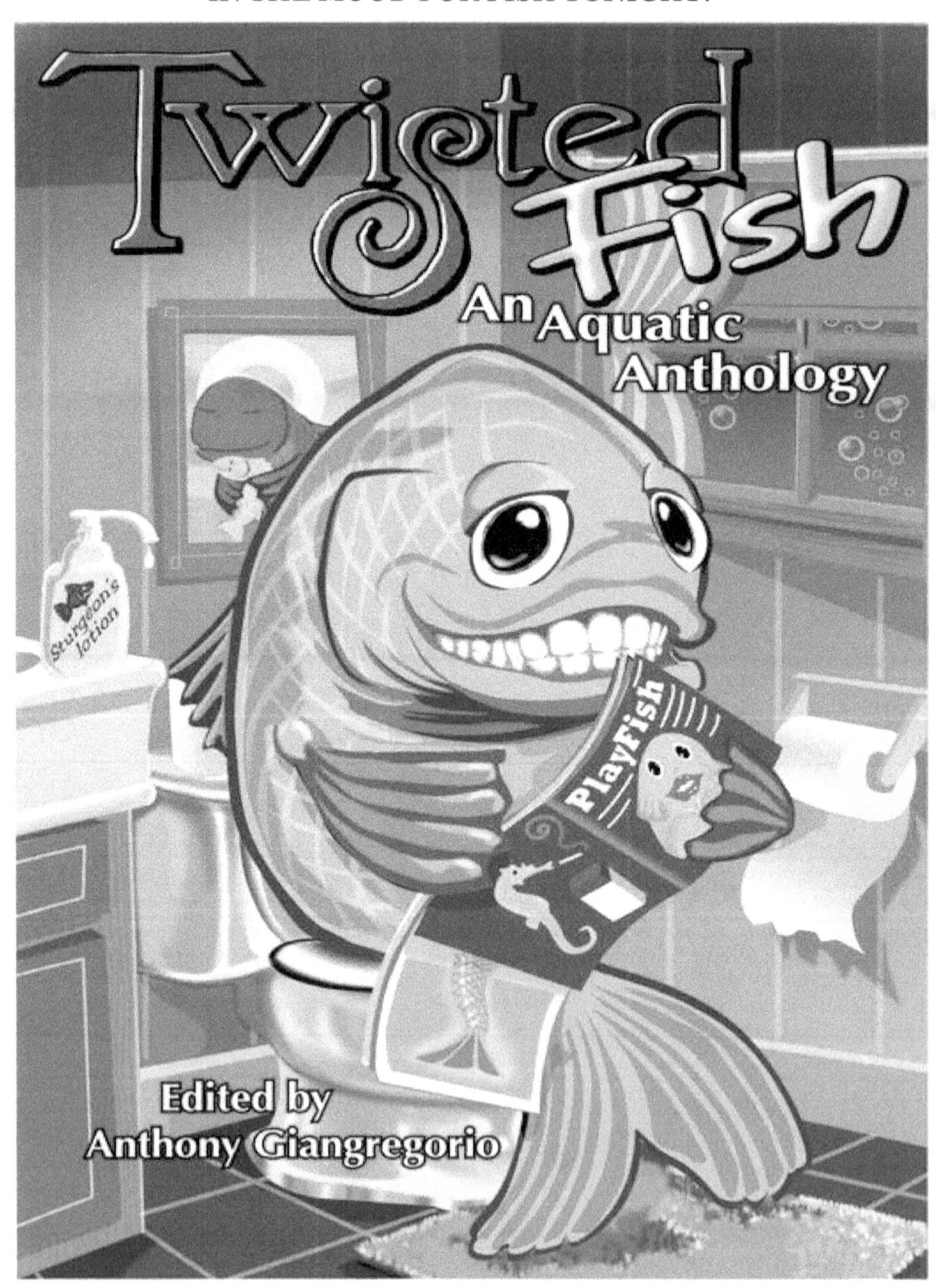

IN THE MOOD FOR FISH TONIGHT?
Twisted Fish
An Aquatic Anthology
Sturgeon's lotion
PlayFish
Edited by
Anthony Giangregorio

PLAYING GOD: A ZOMBIE NOVEL
by Jeffery Dye

It was supposed to be a regeneration virus to help soldiers on the battle-field—regrowing limbs and healing wounds— but a simple act of carelessness unleashed it on an unsuspecting world.

For the virus was not perfected, and once exposed, the host quickly dies, only to rise again as one of the undead.

As countries are quickly overrun, scientists and military teams battle to contain the outbreak.

There is no other option.

If the infection continues to spread, soon the entire globe will be consumed. And perhaps that will be a just punishment for a mankind that dared to try to play God.

DEAD HOUSE: A ZOMBIE GHOST STORY
by Keith Adam Luethke

The old mansion on the edge of town, aptly named Dead House, has a history of blood, pain, and death, but what Victor Leeds knows of this past only scratches the surface of the true horrors within.

But when his girlfriend is attacked by a shadowy figure one rainy night, he soon finds himself caught up in a world where the dead walk and ghostly wraiths abound. And to make matters worse, a pair of serial killers are fulfilling carefully made plans, and when they are done, the small town of Stormville, New York will run red. The last ingredient to open the gates of Hell, and plunge this small upstate town into madness, is rain.

And in Stormville, it pours by the gallons.

The Lazarus Culture
by Pasquale J. Morrone

Secret Service Agent Christopher Kearns had no idea what he was up against. Assigned on a temporary basis to the Center for Disease Control, he only knew that somehow it was connected to the lives of those the agency pro-tected...namely, the President of the United States. If there were possible terrorist activities in the making, he could only guess it was at a red alert basis.

When Kearns meets and befriends Doctor Marlene Peterson of the Breezy Point Medical Center in Maryland, he soon finds that science fiction can indeed become a reality. In a solitary room walked a man with no vital signs: dead. The explanation he received came from Doctor Lee Fret, a man assigned to the case from the CDC. Something was attached to the brain stem. Something alive that was quickly spreading rapidly through Maryland and other states.

Kearns and his ragtag army of agents and medical personnel soon find them-selves in a world of meaningless slaughter and mayhem. The armies of the walking dead were far more than mere zombies. Some began to change into whatever it was they ate. The government had found a way to reanimate the dead by implanting a parasite found on the tongue of the Red Snapper to the human brain. It looked good on paper, but it was a project straight from Hell. The dead now walked, but it wasn't a mystery. It was The Lazarus Culture.

DEAD RAGE

by Anthony Giangregorio
Book 2 in the Rage virus series!

An unknown virus spreads across the globe, turning ordinary people into bloodthirsty, ravenous killers.

Only a small percentage of the population is immune and soon become prey to the infected.

Amongst the infected comes a man, stricken by the virus, yet still retaining his grasp on reality. His need to destroy the *normals* becomes an obsession and he raises an army of killers to seek out and kill all who aren't *changed* like himself. A few survivors gather together on the outskirts of Chicago and find themselves running for their lives as the specter of death looms over all.

The Dead Rage virus will find you, no matter where you hide.

CHRISTMAS IS DEAD: A ZOMBIE ANTHOLOGY

Edited by Anthony Giangregorio

Twas the night before Christmas and all through the house, not a creature was stirring, not even a. . . zombie?

That's right; this anthology explores what would happen at Christmas time if there was a full blown zombie outbreak. Reanimated turkeys, zombie Santas, and demon reindeers that turn people into flesh-eating ghouls are just some of the tales you will find in this merry undead book. So curl up under the Christmas tree with a cup of hot chocolate, and as the fireplace crackles with warmth, get ready to have your heart filled with holiday cheer. But of course, then it will be ripped from your heaving chest and fed upon by blood-thirsty elves with a craving for human flesh! For you see, Christmas is Dead!

And you will never look at the holiday season the same way again.

BLOOD RAGE

(The Prequel to DEAD RAGE)

by Anthony Giangregorio

The madness descended before anyone knew what was happening. Perfectly normal people suddenly became rage-fueled killers, tearing and slicing their way across the city. Within hours, Chicago was a battlefield, the dead strewn in the streets like trash.

Stacy, Chad and a few others are just a few of the immune, unaffected by the virus but not to the violence surrounding them. The *changed* are ravenous, sweeping across Chicago and perhaps the world, destroying any *normals* they come across. Fire, slaughter, and blood rule the land, and the few survivors are now an endangered species.

This is the story of the first days of the Dead Rage virus and the brave souls who struggle to live just one more day.

When the smoke clears, and the *changed* have maimed and killed all who stand in their way, only the strong will remain.

The rest will be left to rot in the sun.

THE BOOK OF CANNIBALS

Edited by Anthony Giangregorio

Human meat . . . the ultimate taboo.

Deep down, in the dark recesses of your mind, can you honestly say you never wondered how it might taste?

Honestly, never wondered if a chunk of thigh tasted like chicken or pork?

Or if a hunk of an arm was similar to steak? And what kind of wine would be served with it, red or white?

Would a human liver be no different than one from a cow, or a pig?

For all we know, human flesh is as tender as veal, better than the finest tenderloin. And that is what the stories in this book are about, eating each other. But be warned, after reading these tales of mastication, you may just become a vegetarian, or at the very least, think twice before taking your first bite of that juicy steak at your local restaurant.

THE TURNING: A STORY OF THE LIVING DEAD

by Kelly M. Hudson

The Dead Walk!

And no place on earth is safe from their ravening hunger. Civilization falls, leaving groups of struggling survivors to navigate a world that has descended into Hell.

Jeff Richards is one such survivor. He and his lover Jenny flee their home in the Bay Area and take a perilous journey through Northern California into Oregon, seeking shelter in rural areas to avoid both the living dead and that most treacherous animal of all: their fellow humans.

But can a man who has lost everything, including his humanity, ever be reborn? When the dead walk, will any of us survive?

Or will we all join the ranks of the undead to forever walk the earth.

VISIONS OF THE DEAD: A ZOMBIE STORY

by Anthony & Joseph Giangregorio

Jake Roberts felt like he was the luckiest man alive.

He had a great family, a beautiful girlfriend, who was soon to be his wife, and a job, that might not have been the best, but it paid the bills.

At least until the dead began to walk.

Now Jake is fighting to survive in a dead world while searching for his lost love, Melissa, knowing she's out there somewhere.

But the past isn't dead, and as he struggles for an uncertain future, the past threatens to consume him. With the present a constant battle between the living and the dead, Jake finds himself slipping in and out of the past, the visions of how it all happened haunting him. But Jake knows Melissa is out there somewhere and he'll find her or die trying.

In a world of the living dead, you can never escape your past.

DEAD MOURNING: A ZOMBIE HORROR STORY
by Anthony Giangregorio

Carl Jenkins was having a run of bad luck. Fresh out of jail, his probation tenuous, he'd lost every job he'd taken since being released. So now was his last chance, only one more job to prevent him from going back to prison. Assigned to work in a funeral home, he accidentally loses a shipment of embalming fluid. With nothing to lose, he substitutes it with a batch of chemicals from a nearby factory.

The results don't go as planned, though. While his screw-up goes unnoticed, his machinations revive the cadavers in the funeral home, unleashing an evil on the world that it has not seen before. Not wanting to become a snack for the rampaging dead, he flees the city, joining up with other survivors. An old, dilapidated zoo becomes their haven, while the dead wait outside the walls, hungry and patient.

But Carl is optimistic, after all, he's still alive, right? Perhaps his luck has changed and help will arrive to save them all?

Unfortunately, unknown to him and the other survivors, a serial killer has fallen into their group, trapped inside the zoo with them.

With the undead army clamoring outside the walls and a murderer within, it'll be a miracle if any of them live to see the next sunrise.

On second thought, maybe Carl would've been better off if he'd just gone back to jail.

ROAD KILL: A ZOMBIE TALE
by Anthony Giangregorio

In the summer of 2008, a rogue comet entered earth's orbit for 72 hours. During this time, a strange amber glow suffused the sky.

But something else happened; something in the comet's tail had an adverse affect on dead tissue and the result was the reanimation of every dead animal carcass on the planet.

A handful of survivors hole up in a diner in the backwoods of New Hampshire while the undead creatures of the night hunt for human prey.

There's a new blue plate special at DJ's Diner and Truck Stop, and it's you!

DEAD THINGS
by Anthony Giangregorio

Beneath the veil of reality we all know as truth, there is another world, one where creatures only seen in nightmares exist.

But what if these creatures do actually exist, and it is us that are only fleeting images, mere visions conjured up by some unknown being.

Werewolves, zombies, vampires, and other lost things that go bump in the night, inhabit the world of imagination and myth, but all will be found in this collection of tales. But in this world, fiction becomes fact, and what lurks in the shadows is real. Beware the next time you sense you are being watched or catch movement in the corner of your eye, for though it may be nothing, it might just be your doom.

THE DARK

by Anthony Giangregorio

DARKNESS FALLS

The darkness came without warning.

First New York, then the rest of United States, and then the world became enveloped in a perpetual night without end.

With no sunlight, eventually the planet will wither and die, bringing on a new Ice Age. But that isn't problem for the human race, for humanity will be dead long before that happens.

There is something in the dark, creatures only seen in nightmares, and they are on the prowl. Evolution has changed and man is no longer the dominant species. When we are children, we're told not to fear the dark, that what we believe to exist in the shadows is false.

Unfortunately, that is no longer true.

SOULEATER

by Anthony Giangregorio

Twenty years ago, Jason Lawson witnessed the brutal death of his father by something only seen in nightmares, something so horrible he'd blocked it from his mind.

Now twenty years later the creature is back, this time for his son.

Jason won't let that happen.

He'll travel to the demon's world, struggling every second to rescue his son from its clutches.

But what he doesn't know is that the portal will only be open for a finite time and if he doesn't return with his son before it closes, then he'll be trapped in the demon's dimension forever.

SEE HOW IT ALL BEGAN IN THE NEW DOUBLE-SIZED 460 PAGE SPECIAL EDITION!

DEADWATER: EXPANDED EDITION

by Anthony Giangregorio

Through a series of tragic mishaps, a small town's water supply is contaminated with a deadly bacterium that transforms the town's population into flesh eating ghouls.

Without warning, Henry Watson finds himself thrown into a living hell where the living dead walk and want nothing more than to feed on the living.

Now Henry's trying to escape the undead town before he becomes the next victim.

With the military on one side, shooting civilians on sight, and a horde of bloodthirsty zombies on the other, Henry must try to battle his way to freedom.

With a small group of survivors, including a beautiful secretary and a wise-cracking janitor to aid him, the ragtag group will do their best to stay alive and escape the city codenamed: **Deadwater**.

DEAD END: A ZOMBIE NOVEL
by Anthony Giangregorio
THE DEAD WALK!

Newspapers everywhere proclaim the dead have returned to feast on the living!

A small group of survivors hole up in a cellar, afraid to brave the masses of animated corpses, but when food runs out, they have no choice but to venture out into a world gone mad.

What they will discover, however, is that the fall of civilization has brought out the worst in their fellow man. Cannibals, psychotic preachers and rapists are just some of the atrocities they must face.

In a world turned upside down, it is life that has hit a Dead End.

BOOK OF THE DEAD 2: NOT DEAD YET
A ZOMBIE ANTHOLOGY
Edited by Anthony Giangregorio

Out of the ashes of death and decay, comes the second volume filled with the walking dead.

In this tomb, there are only slow, shambling monstrosities that were once human.

No one knows why the dead walk; only that they do, and that they are hungry for human flesh.

But these aren't your neighbors, your co-workers, or your family.
Now they are the living dead, and they will tear your throat out at a moment's notice. So be warned as you delve into the pages of this book; the dead will find you, no matter where you hide.

ZOMBIES IN OUR HOMETOWN
By Gary Wedlund

All Joe Jefferson wants to do is go fishing.

But little does he know, three days later he'll be leading a ragtag group of survivors through a zombie-infested town. A mortician's skin treatment has done its job a little too well. Aunt Millie makes a miraculous recovery and goes on a murderous rampage, to the amazement of the mourners.

Friends, relatives, the mortician, and even the televangelist, Reverend Purswell, are left to sort out the leftovers.

Nobody knows what the mess is all about until confronted with the exponentially born again. As more of the recently deceased munch on the town, the police have one idea about how to confront the zombies, and the Reverend Purswell another.

While everyone is engaged with tom-foolery, Officer Sandra Anderson and Joe get to the bottom of the horror, one grave encounter at a time.

Not much of a first date.

Will they ever get to a simple dinner and movie?

INSIDE THE PERIMETER: SCAVENGERS OF THE DEAD
by Alan Spencer

In the middle of nowhere, the vestiges of an abandoned town are surrounded by inescapably high concrete barriers, permitting no trespass or escape. The town is dormant of human life, but rampant with the living dead, who choose not to eat flesh, but to instead continue their survival by cruder means.

Boyd Broman, a detective arrested and falsely imprisoned, has been transferred into the secret town. He is given an ultimatum: recapture Hayden Grubaugh, the cannibal serial killer, who has been banished to the town, in exchange for his freedom.

During Boyd's search, he discovers why the psychotic cannibal must really be captured and the sinister secrets the dead town holds.

With no chance of escape, Broman finds himself trapped among the ravenous, violent dead.

With the cannibal feeding on the animated cadavers and the undead searching for Boyd, he must fulfill his end of the deal before the rotting corpses turn him into an unwilling organ donor.

But Boyd wasn't told that no one gets out alive, that the town is a death sentence.

For there is no escape from *Inside the Perimeter*.

DEADFALL
by Anthony Giangregorio

It's Halloween in the small suburban town of Wakefield, Mass.

While parents take their children trick or treating and others throw costume parties, a swarm of meteorites enter the earth's atmosphere and crash to earth.

Inside are small parasitic worms, no larger than maggots.

The worms quickly infect the corpses at a local cemetery and so begins the rise of the undead.

The walking dead soon get the upper hand, with no one believing the truth. That the dead now walk.

Will a small group of survivors live through the zombie apocalypse?

Or will they, too, succumb to the Deadfall.

LOVE IS DEAD: A ZOMBIE ANTHOLOGY
Edited by Anthony Giangregorio
THE DEATH OF LOVE

Valentine's Day is a day when young love is fulfilled.

Where hopeful young men bring candy and flowers to their sweethearts, in hopes of a kiss...or perhaps more. But not in this anthology.

For you see, LOVE IS DEAD, and in this tome, the dead walk, wanting to feed on those same hearts that once pumped in chests, bursting with love.

So toss aside that heart-shaped box of candy and throw away those red roses, you won't need them any longer. Instead, strap on a handgun, or pick up a shotgun and defend yourself from the ravenous undead.

Because in a world where the dead walk, even love isn't safe.

UNITED STATES OF ARMAGEDDON
by Jeffrey Thomas Crooms
THE END OF A COUNTRY!

America's enemies plot a sadistic plan to destroy the population and armed forces so they can swoop in and rule the country.

Terrorists called the Horsemen smuggle in a deadly biological weapon straight to the heart of the United States and release it.

The result is a land covered with corpses, bloated bodies strewn from sea to sea.

A few desperate survivors battle through the blighted landscape on a last ditch mission to save the country from total domination.

But the biological weapon has a side effect, one no one would have ever foreseen, one too unimaginable to even contemplate.

Welcome to the future. Welcome to the Unite States of *Armageddon*

BOOK OF THE DEAD
A ZOMBIE ANTHOLOGY VOL 1
ISBN 978-1-935458-25-8
Edited by Anthony Giangregorio

This is the most faithful, truest zombie anthology ever written, and we invite you along for the ride. Every single story in this book is filled with slack-jawed, eyes glazed, slow moving, shambling zombies set in a world where the dead have risen and only want to eat the flesh of the living. In these pages, the rules are sacrosanct. There is no deviation from what a zombie should be or how they came about. The Dead Walk.

There is no reason, though rumors and suppositions fill the radio and television stations. But the only thing that is fact is that the walking dead are here and they will not go away. So prepare yourself for the ultimate homage to the master of zombie legend. And remember... Aim for the head!

REVOLUTION OF THE DEAD
by Anthony Giangregorio
THE DEAD SHALL RISE AGAIN!

Five years ago, a deadly plague wiped out 97% of the world's population, America suffering tragically. Bodies were everywhere, far too many to bury or burn. But then, through a miracle of medical science, a way is found to reanimate the dead.

With the manpower of the United States depleted, and the remaining survivors not wanting to give up their internet and fast food restaurants, the undead are conscripted as slave labor.

Now they cut the grass, pick up the trash, and walk the dogs of the surviving humans.

But whether alive or dead, no race wants to be controlled, and sooner or later the dead will fight back, wanting the freedom they enjoyed in life.

The revolution has begun!

And when it's over, the dead will rule the land, and the remaining humans will become the slaves...or worse.

KINGDOM OF THE DEAD
by Anthony Giangregorio
THE DEAD HAVE RISEN!

In the dead city of Pittsburgh, two small enclaves struggle to survive, eking out an existence of hand to mouth.

But instead of working together, both groups battle for the last remaining fuel and supplies of a city filled with the living dead.

Six months after the initial outbreak, a lone helicopter arrives bearing two more survivors and a newborn baby. One enclave welcomes them, while the other schemes to steal their helicopter and escape the decaying city.

With no police, fire, or social services existing, the two will battle for dominance in the steel city of the walking dead. But when the dust settles, the question is: will the remaining humans be the winners, or the losers?

When the dead walk, the line between Heaven and Hell is so twisted and bent there is no line at all.

RISE OF THE DEAD
by Anthony Giangregorio
DEATH IS ONLY THE BEGINNING!

In less than forty-eight hours, more than half the globe was infected.

In another forty-eight, the rest would be enveloped.

The reason?

A science experiment gone horribly wrong which enabled the dead to walk, their flesh rotting on their bones even as they seek human prey.

Jeremy was an ordinary nineteen year old slacker. He partied too much and had done poorly in high school. After a night of drinking and drugs, he awoke to find the world a very different place from the one he'd left the night before.

The dead were walking and feeding on the living, and as Jeremy stepped out into a world gone mad, the dead spotting him alone and unarmed in the middle of the street, he had to wonder if he would live long enough to see his twentieth birthday.

THE CHRONICLES OF JACK PRIMUS
BOOK ONE
by Michael D. Griffiths

Beneath the world of normalcy we all live in lies another world, one where supernatural beings exist.

These creatures of the night hunt us; want to feed on our very souls, though only a few know of their existence.

One such man is Jack Primus, who accidentally pierces the veil between this world and the next. With no other choice if he wants to live, he finds himself on the run, hunted by beings called the Xemmoni, an ancient race that sees humans as nothing but cattle. They want his soul, to feed on his very essence, and they will kill all who stand in their way. But if they thought Jack would just lie down and accept his fate, they were sorely mistaken. He didn't ask for this battle, but he knew he would fight them with everything at his disposal, for to lose is a fate worse than death.

He would win this war, and he would take down anyone who got in his way.

THE WAR AGAINST THEM: A ZOMBIE NOVEL
by Jose Alfredo Vazquez

Mankind wasn't prepared for the onslaught.

An ancient organism is reanimating the dead bodies of its victims, creating worldwide chaos and panic as the disease spreads to every corner of the globe. As governments struggle to contain the disease, courageous individuals across the planet learn what it truly means to make choices as they struggle to survive.

Geopolitics meet technology in a race to save mankind from the worst threat it has ever faced. Doctors, military and soldiers from all walks of life battle to find a cure. For the dead walk, and if not stopped, they will wipe out all life on Earth. Humanity is fighting a war they cannot win, for who can overcome Death itself? Man versus the walking dead with the winner ruling the planet. Welcome to *The War Against Them*.

DEADTOWN: A DEADWATER STORY
B OOK 8
by Anthony Giangregorio

The world is a very different place now. The dead walk the land and humans hide in small towns with walls of stone and debris for protection, constantly keeping the living dead at bay.

Social law is gone and right and wrong is defined by the size of your gun.

UNWELCOME VISITORS

Henry Watson and his band of warrior survivalists become guests in a fortified town in Michigan. But when the kidnapping of one of the companions goes bad and men die, the group finds themselves on the wrong side of the law, and a town out for blood.

Trapped in a hotel, surrounded on all sides, it will be up to Henry to save the day with a gamble that may not only take his life, but that of his friends as well.

In a dead world, when justice is not enough, there is always vengeance.

END OF DAYS: AN APOCALYPTIC ANTHOLOGY
VOLUMES 1-4
Edited by Anthony Giangregorio

Our world is a fragile place.

Meteors, famine, floods, nuclear war, solar flares, and hundreds of other calamities can plunge our small blue planet into turmoil in an instant.

What would you do if tomorrow the sun went super nova or the world was swallowed by water, submerging the world into the cold darkness of the ocean? This anthology explores some of those scenarios and plunges you into total annihilation.

But remember, it's only a book, and tomorrow will come as it always does. Or will it?

KNIGHT SYNDROME: TEMPLARS OF THE UNDEAD
by Jesus Riddle Morales

A young nun is commissioned to find the Pope's abducted daughter, but quickly realizes she is part of a bloodline of reincarnated saints, destined to fight against an evil relic that empowers creatures from beyond the grave.

Soon, she is thrown into a world she only dreamed of, filled with demons from her nightmares. With her very life hanging in the balance, she will battle the hordes of Hell, for if she fails, the consequences will be dire.

www.ingramcontent.com/pod-product-compliance
Lightning Source LLC
Chambersburg PA
CBHW070949180726
48291CB00004B/1215